I Trust Her Completely

I Trust Her Completely

A NOVEL

Christine Henneberg

ISBN 979-8-9860667-2-1 Paperback

ISBN 979-8-9860667-3-8 Ebook

Library of Congress Control Number: 2025901580

For S & S
and
for Mo

PART ONE

M Y FIRST PREGNANCY was an everyday accident, an ordinary disaster. I remember it—the parallel blue lines, the drops of urine on my thumb—the way you would remember a car crash: in bright, jagged pieces. The crunch of metal and the slash of the seat belt across your waist. The airbag exploding into the tiny bones around your eyeballs. A sort of numb, helpless passivity. Even though I was physically present for every moment, I would have said, without irony, that I didn't totally understand how it happened.

I think a lot about the counterfactual. *What if this? What if that?* The things that happen, and the things that don't. When I was a teenager, my parents died suddenly, both at once. So you think about those kinds of things.

I never calculated the exact due date, though, or passed the subsequent years thinking about how old the baby, the child, would have been. I remember the month and the season of that pregnancy only by the crisp sensory details around the edges: The morning sunlight on the surface of the pool. The weight of a book in my backpack: *A Portrait of the Artist as a Young Man.* The thin blue sweater with the sleeves that bunched around my elbows. The flurry of wisteria blossoms on the sidewalk.

I can see now, better than I could at the time, how lucky I was. Had I not made the choice I did, my life would have changed dramatically in ways that probably wouldn't have worked out well for anyone. But that's the kind of thing we rarely stop to think about, or at least I didn't back then: the day nothing changed. Like the improbable survivor who emerges unscathed from the wreckage, there I was, shaken but intact, more or less the same person I was before. Except for one thing: I had Radhika.

But not for long. After college, the next time I would see her was seventeen years later, in a Safeway in San Francisco where I was shopping for, of all things, a pregnancy test.

1

I THOUGHT YOU were dead."

They were the first words out of my mouth, after her name. What a thing to say to someone you haven't seen in almost twenty years. Actually, by then I'd known for over a month that she was very much alive, and that she was somewhere in San Francisco. I'd read it in the magazine. But I guess I didn't quite believe it. I still remember the shock and the thrill I felt that day: Nothing was what I'd thought it was. Everything might still change.

I spotted her a few steps ahead of me in the pharmacy aisle, peering at the cough-cold shelf with the intent gaze of someone who knows exactly what she's looking for. She wore green scrubs and an expensive-looking black coat belted at the waist. She seemed taller. Her short hair was fashionably tousled on her narrow head.

"Radhika."

I thought she might not recognize or even remember me. But her face broke into a luminous smile and she said,

"Josie." She dropped whatever she was holding into her cart and wrapped her arms around me. She smelled like hospital soap and bergamot.

I whispered it into her shoulder, my eyes squeezed shut, the way you'd confess the dark, vivid details of a nightmare: "I thought you were dead." She tossed her head back and laughed, showing her pretty throat. "Not me. Not yet." Her eyes were fierce and brilliant. She held me in front of her like a doll: skinny neck and shoulders, glasses, pale freckles, dripping ponytail smelling faintly of chlorine. "You haven't changed," she said. And in a way she was right; I hadn't.

Then she said quietly, "I've thought about you so much."

For a long time I wondered what she meant by this. What made her think of me, and when? What was there to think about?

I said, "I've thought about you, too."

I fell into step beside her as she barreled down the aisle and into conversation, loading sensible groceries into her cart with the particular satisfaction of a mother deciding what her family will eat (bagged bagels, baby carrots) and what they won't (junk cereals, juice). I noticed she placed certain items that seemed to be meant just for her (Manchego cheese, chocolate-covered almonds, apple cider vinegar) in the top of the cart, as though to keep them separate and safe.

She went through the checkout line first, collecting her long, elegant receipt like a prize. I followed with my little basket. It was the day after Halloween and there were still bags of candy piled by the counter. As the cashier ran the pregnancy test over the scanner with a cursory red beep, I watched to see if Radhika had noticed. She hadn't. She was still talking, leaning over her cart, her long body bending like a sunflower on its stalk. They lived in Laurel Heights, just two blocks from here, she said. She worked a few miles away, at UCSF, where she was an Associate Professor of Obstetrics & Gynecology in the Family Planning department. I asked (although I already knew) what exactly this meant: "family planning." She explained that she was a doctor who specialized in abortions and miscarriages. She cared for the women whose pregnancies, for whatever reason, would never become babies.

"Of course. That makes so much sense," I said, feigning delighted surprise. She beamed with the satisfaction of a young talent fulfilling her early recognized potential. I noticed how she'd said the word *abortion* without so much as a glance at the cashier or the other shoppers in line behind us.

She did not ask about me, which was fine. At that moment I wasn't ready to tell her the truth: that exactly two weeks and two days earlier I'd been on my back, hips tilted to the ceiling, while a nurse practitioner inserted a long syringe into my vagina. (The NP told me afterward that I had a "very small and mobile cervix," an odd description that made my anatomy sound like a compact car.) The clinic had offered to test my blood for pregnancy hormones as soon as ten days afterward, but I'd told them I would test at home. I'd been putting it off. So far I felt perfectly, physiologically unchanged. If the procedure had worked, I would have a baby in the first week of July. If not, my life would continue just as it had been. I could accept either possibility, was even enjoying that state of blissful, extended-yet-ephemeral suspense, when anything could still happen.

And yet it all felt too close to what had happened in the past, and to Radhika's present area of expertise, to tell her. But I must've known she would find out. Of course she would.

"I wish I could bring you to our house so we could catch up properly." She paused near the Wells Fargo counter, still talking, apparently unconcerned about her melting frozen peas. "But unfortunately we're hosting a Día de los Muertos party at our house right now, with all our kids' little friends. Our amazing nanny put the whole thing together." She shot me a guilty look. "I was actually sort of hoping to miss it. But of course, today of all days, Labor & Delivery is completely empty, and I'm off early."

"Ah," I said. "Hence the leisurely trip to the grocery store."

"Exactly!" She glanced ruefully at her half dozen bags, nestled in the cart like eggs in a nest. "But even this must come to an end."

Feeling suddenly panicked at the thought of her leaving, I said, "I actually kind of like kids' parties."

I've always thought one reason people appreciate having me around is that I'm quick to go along with what others want. This makes it seem like I don't really care one way or another what happens, like I'll be happy however things turn out. But that's not true. I care very much about how things turn out. I want things to go well, and right. It's just that I don't often trust that I'm the best person to make that happen. How can you ever be sure one way is the right way? What if another way might be better? I suppose you could say I'm easily swayed by other people's suggestions, by alternative possibilities. The kind of person who will happily tag along on someone else's weekend plans.

Radhika shot me a sort of sly, bemused look. "Really?"

I shrugged. "Really."

THE LATE AFTERNOON was already turning toward dusk when we pulled up to Radhika's house, a large Edwardian on a quiet corner. Lit up like a jewel box with landscape lights, jack-o'-lantern grinning on the porch, and paper lanterns lining the walkways and windows, it looked like something from the pages of a children's book. But it was clearly a grown-up house, with a manicured low-water landscape, Japanese maples flanking the sides, a stately knocker stuck on a royal blue front door. A pale half-moon hung over the roof like a good omen.

The garage door whirred open and we pulled in. Radhika pointed me to an enormous spare fridge, its shelves empty except for a case of Pellegrino and an unopened jar of Dijon mustard. I shoved my single grocery bag inside.

From a narrow hallway off the garage, I thought she would lead me through one of the two doors on either side, but she pointed up a flight of stairs. "Brace yourself for the chaos."

At the top of the stairway was a laundry room that opened into a lustrous kitchen: wide countertops glowing under banks of recessed lighting, stainless steel appliances, glass-fronted cabinets. On the other side of the counter, ten small children sat around a table covered in newspaper, paintbrushes in hand, heads bowed over plaster skulls, little brows furrowed in concentration. A few glanced up at us. Two smiling faces landed on Radhika. "Mama!"

She waggled her fingers at them. "Those are my two. Sachin and Saniya." She sounded bemused, almost bored, but also proud.

A deep, genial voice said, "They've been asking about you." A man touched a possessive hand to the small of Radhika's back. His other hand landed, firm and welcoming, on my shoulder. I turned to look at him: tall, squarely built, handsome in the most unsurprising way. Adam. She leaned coyly, almost imperceptibly, into his hand, the chemistry between them arresting yet contained. For the briefest moment they stood there like that, stunning in their physical perfection, gazing upon their two beautiful children.

The girl, Saniya, looked like Radhika, with dark skin, long lashes, and thick black hair cut short around a heart-shaped face. Sachin was a head taller than his sister, even seated. His shoulders were wide and boyishly athletic, and he had a bony jaw and deep-set eyes that made him look almost distinguished. His skin was fair, his hair a fine chestnut brown. He was not so obviously Indian, could even have passed as white—his father's son.

But Radhika and Adam were not the type of parents to stand there admiring their own offspring for long. "Have you been scrounging up party guests from the streets?" he said to her with a wink, then stepped back just enough to extend both arms, gripping my hand in his. Here was a man who clearly knew the splendor of his smile. And yet there was something unexpectedly humble, even vulnerable in his eyes. They told me everything I needed to know: he loved Radhika, and by extension he loved any friend of hers.

"Josie's a dear friend from college." Radhika gave my shoulders a little squeeze, and for a glorious moment I felt myself at the center of their combined, bodily attention. "We were serendipitously reunited in Safeway, of all places, and I convinced her to come over. Even though I warned her it would mean facing this zoo." She flung a hand toward the skull-painting party.

Adam bestowed his smile on me once more and released my hand. "Brave of you to come, Josie. Even Radhika tried to get out of this one." She gave him a jab in the ribs with her pointed elbow. Through a wincing grin he said, "Mercy's got the kids in the palm of her hand, as usual." He gestured toward the head of the table, where a young, dark-haired woman sat painting a skull and chatting with the children at her sides. I stared at her. She was girlishly athletic in jeans and flip flops, the sleeves of her white T-shirt rolled up to show her muscled arms. A few dark curls had pulled loose from her ponytail, framing her face: brown skin at her temples, a streak of green paint smudged across one cheek, thick eyebrows that fuzzed together over brown eyes, a small mouth.

"The nanny?" I heard myself ask, almost in a whisper.

Radhika sighed. "Only until July."

"Where will she go in July?"

"Nowhere." She picked up a bottle of white wine and a corkscrew. "We're going to my parents' in Chicago for most of the summer. The kids will start kindergarten when we get back."

"Poor Rad." Adam made a pouting face that wasn't entirely mocking. "She really believes she won't survive without Mercy."

Radhika shook her head. "I've held onto her for too long. I have to let her go."

"And we all know where she'll end up," said a voice behind us. A laughing, heavy-set woman ambled up from the table, where she'd been assisting with the art project. Adam introduced her as Myra, and I could see immediately that she must be Mercy's older sister. They had the same kind brown eyes and round cheeks, but this woman had fine lines at the corners of her mouth, large breasts, and the thick waist of a woman who had born children.

I wondered what she meant: Where was Mercy destined to end up after she left Radhika's house? But I didn't know how to put this question to her. Instead I said, "Which ones are yours?"

She pointed out two girls at the table, also dark-skinned and curly haired, a bit older than Sachin and Saniya. "And yours?" she asked, her voice warm and inclusive.

"Oh, no, I …"

"Josie lives the intellectual life," Radhika said, linking her elbow in mine. "She's a writer."

"Ah. One of your kind," said Myra.

Radhika held out a glass of white wine to me, but I shook my head. "Can I get you something else? A glass of red? A beer?"

"Thanks. I'll stick with water."

She shrugged and sipped from the glass herself. My eyes strayed back to Mercy, who was leaning over the shoulder of one of the children, a crescent of brown hip visible between the top of her jeans and her shirt. She was very young. I turned away, surprised by the dense heat of physical attraction. The feeling was so strong that for a moment I almost forgot about that other, more complicated pull, the reason I was here: Radhika.

WHAT IF I'D never met her? Or what if I'd never run into her that day in Safeway? What if she were still dead? (That was actually how I thought about it: she'd been dead, and now she wasn't anymore.) Not that I wished this. But part of me wished, even then, that I could go back to when I'd still believed it.

Of course it's never that simple. The counterfactual: *What if this, what if that?* That's not a story. If I hadn't read Radhika's essay, then I might never have tried to get pregnant in the first place. And if I hadn't seen her that day in Safeway, then I never would've met Mercy. These were harder realities to wish away, even as an experiment.

Nevertheless, there was a way in which I felt cheated. All along it had been something I was supposed to do alone, with no one else's help. That was the whole point. Radhika's influence had been at work from the beginning, and I knew it. But for that brief sliver of time, while my grocery bag was still tucked in the cold, dark cavern of Radhika's fridge, my decisions and their consequences belonged entirely to me. That secret uncertainty, the solitary unknown. I loved that feeling. I still sometimes long for it.

2

AFTER CUPCAKES AND a piñata everyone migrated to the front door to say their goodbyes. "But not you, Josie." Radhika circled her long fingers around my wrist. "You're not going anywhere."

Within ten minutes the house was empty. Mercy had disappeared, I didn't know where. Adam was hustling the twins upstairs for their baths. Radhika and I sat at the kitchen table, a bouquet of paintbrushes soaking in a mason jar on the counter, a row of painted skulls watching us from the windowsill.

Before she could open her mouth, I told her, "Rad. I read your essay."

"Oh! That essay. It was good of you to read it." She'd sliced an apple for us to share and made a pot of tea. Now she looked up from pouring the tea into two mugs.

"It was … incredible," I said. "I learned so much about you. And there's so much more I want to know."

"Well, you're going to get your wish. I got a book deal out of that essay."

I swallowed. "You're writing a book?"

"Yeah, like I didn't have enough on my plate already. But I'm not complaining. I'm happy, obviously." She pushed a mug toward me that read: Of All the Vaginas in the World, I'm So Glad I Tumbled out of Yours. Happy Mother's Day!

I pointed to the mug. "Did the kids choose that?"

She rolled her eyes. "Adam. He really is the best husband in the world."

I blew on my tea. "So what's the book about?"

"They just want more of what's in the essay: motherhood, abortion, hard choices." She flicked a hand dismissively. "My agent and I came up with a chapter-by-chapter outline. Now I've just got to write it." She looked at me, a smile playing on her lips. "And what about *your* writing? The great novel?"

I shook my head. "I don't know if that's ever going to happen."

"Why not?"

"I guess you could say I have trouble with endings."

"That's funny. I always think of the ending as the easiest part. In college I always used to start with the ending, and then go back and write the rest."

"I guess that's one way to approach it." I was remembering Radhika's short stories in college, their formulaic simplicity. I remembered, too, the detailed notes she scribbled in the margins of my stories, annotating furiously with her red pen until the very last minute of class, and the lengthy, single-spaced critiques stapled to the back.

She peered at me now through narrowed, smiling eyes. "So when can I see it?"

"The novel?"

"Yes, the novel."

"Um, anytime."

"Will you send it tonight? When you get home?"

"Sure," I said, trying my best to sound reluctant. The truth was that I'd been hoping for this: that she would ask about the novel, offer to read it. She'd always been generous in that way—not with praise, but with a willingness to look closely enough at the most flawed and amateur piece of writing to find some merit, even some beauty in it. Radhika's true talent, I'd known even in college, wasn't as a writer. She was an editor.

She actually rubbed her hands together. "I can't wait to read it." Before I could respond with some self-deprecating caveat, she went on. "So what's your process? When do you get your writing done?"

"Early mornings and evenings mostly, after I get home from work and a swim. I write a lot on the weekends."

She grinned. "You're still swimming."

I nodded and told her about the pool at the Jewish Community Center.

"That's just a few blocks from here."

Because I was afraid she'd ask me more about my writing, I started telling her about the late-afternoon JCC crowd: the elderly ladies with their pool noodles, the men with their water-walking belts, the quiet, familiar routine. But I could see she was only half-listening. She seemed deep in thought.

"Hey," she said after a moment. "I've got a great idea." I held my breath. "Why don't we workshop each other's manuscripts? Like in college, only it'll be just the two of us. We can swap our writing back and forth, a little bit at a time. You can finish your novel. And I can write a draft of this damn book."

I felt a brief tug. I thought of my quiet evenings at home with my laptop and my notebooks. The pan cooling on the stove, curling with the lacy edges of a fried egg. The ocean under a blanket of fog. My solitary, beloved writing time.

"It'll be perfect," she went on, breaking me out of my trance. "You're exactly what I need: a writing buddy." I smiled weakly at her. "And"— she gave the back of my hand a little slap—"I'm exactly what *you* need. A cheerleader, someone to read your work and tell you how good it is, and show you how it could be better. Someone to keep telling you you're *going* to finish this novel, you're *going* to publish it, it's going to be great."

"Is that what I need?" I smiled despite myself.

"Yes, it is," she said, and frowned. "And *I* need to finish this book before my deadline."

"When's your deadline?"

She chewed on her lip. "July."

"When your nanny leaves."

"Exactly."

I thought about this for a moment. "That's the publisher's deadline? Or your own deadline?"

"Ha! See how smart you are." She looked at me as though I were a precocious child. Then with a shrug she said, "It's both."

I swallowed. "Rad. There's something else I haven't told you."

I explained all of it: the months of vague longing followed by a sudden certainty, making a point to emphasize the role of her essay in that decisive moment. The fertility clinic (the same one where her own frozen embryos were stored, as it turned out), the hastily chosen sperm donor. I watched her take it all in. I suppose I feared, or maybe hoped, that this news would change everything: who she thought I was, what she thought I was capable of.

She watched me closely as I spoke, listening with her whole body. "Just so I'm clear," she said. "You're doing this alone. Without a partner."

"Yes." My heart pounded in my throat.

"And—you're gay, right?"

"Yes," I said again, then added, "I know it might seem weird, because … I mean, after what happened in college …"

She held up a hand. "Josie. Do you know how many queer pregnant patients I take care of every week? I get it. Nothing in life is simple. Context is everything."

I faltered, feeling at once deeply understood and categorically dismissed. Before I could respond, she said, "So … Are you saying what I think you're saying? Have you actually been sitting here listening to me go on about my stupid book contract for the past hour when you could be *pregnant*? Right *now*?"

I laughed nervously. She clutched her hair in both hands. "I would be going *crazy* if I were you. When we were doing IVF I used to check a pregnancy test approximately four times a day." This was one of the great paradoxes I would come to know about Radhika: I often got the feeling, and later she even said so herself, that she didn't particularly like being a mother. And yet it seemed—at least that night, and over the next few months—that nothing would make her happier than for me to become a mother, too.

She leaned back in her chair. "You know, at work we've got pregnancy tests lying around everywhere. I find them in the bottom of my purse the way other people find ballpoint pens." I laughed, but she looked me straight in the eye. "I'm serious. Do you want me to see if I've got one?"

"Actually," I said, smiling a little, "I have one in my grocery bag."

She leaned forward and grabbed my shoulders. "In my *fridge?*"

I blushed and laughed, beaming in the glow of her excitement.

"Go check!"

"Now?"

"Why not? When did you say your insemination was?"

"Sixteen days ago."

"Josie." She pulled me toward her, looking straight into my eyes. "*What are you waiting for?*" She pointed to a door off the kitchen. "The bathroom is right there."

That was how I learned, for the second time in my life, that I was pregnant: the same two blue lines, the clear drops of urine on my thumb. Only this time, instead of vomiting in a dorm room wastebasket, I lay the white plastic stick face up on Radhika's porcelain sink, washed my hands, and opened the door. I called out to her.

3

WHEN RADHIKA WAS in medical school and I was getting my graduate degree in fiction writing, I used to send her drafts of my short stories. Though she must have been incredibly busy, she always responded, sometimes on the same day. Her astute comments and suggestions were more helpful than anything I could have gotten from my classmates, even from most of my professors.

She assured me she loved doing this. It kept alive a part of her brain that would otherwise slowly wither away in medical school. "I miss thinking about words and stories. I'm *jealous* of you, Josie, truth be told. It turns out medicine isn't for the faint of heart."

This sounded like false modesty to me. Who would ever call Radhika "the faint of heart"?

Somewhat to my surprise, the story collection I completed as a master's thesis won a First Book Award with a small, reputable press in New Mexico. The stories all dealt with the same themes: a young girl who had lost her ambitious, energetic parents to a terrible accident, the vacuum of what it meant to go on living in their absence.

I wrote to Radhika immediately:

Hi Rad. Good news: Some stories I wrote won a small prize and are going to be published—my first book! (Not a novel yet. Maybe someday ...) Can I ask you a huge favor? My editor and I are going through one more round of revisions before publication. I want it to be as good as it can be. Would you read the complete manuscript and tell me what you think?

A full two months passed. While I waited for her reply I fiddled with the text, making small edits here and there. I truly believed I would hear from her. When my editor nudged me for a third time asking for my final edits, I wrote to her again.

Hi Radhika,
It's been a while. You must be getting ready to graduate from med school. A brief update: the book is done and ready for publication! So please don't worry about my earlier request to read it. I'll send you a copy when it comes out. In the meantime, when you have a moment, please tell me about what's going on in your life. I've been thinking of you.
Your friend,
Josie

This time she responded within an hour:

Josie,

Thanks for your note, and sorry for being out of touch.

It turns out I have breast cancer—the bad kind, or so they tell me. So life has been sort of upside-down. The Ob-Gyn residency director at Northwestern is holding a spot for me, hopefully for next year. In the meantime my family and my boyfriend, Adam, are tremendous sources of support. Naturally I plan to fight with all I've got, and hope to be back to my usual self before too long.

Josie, congratulations on the book. I'm sure it'll be a smashing success.

xoxo

Rad

I hit REPLY and sat staring at the blank email window. I thought of how impatient and self-centered I'd been, sitting here all these weeks waiting for Radhika's praise and congratulations, wondering if I'd done something to upset or offend her. I thought of all the things I could write to her now: that I owed the completion of this book to her, that in a way I felt my life was inseparable from hers, tangled up in a knot of admiration and appreciation and need. But it all seemed inadequate and too much at the same time. She had her family, and her boyfriend. She was a doctor, or practically a doctor. What could she possibly need from me?

I wrote the shortest, simplest note I could, telling her I would be thinking of her. I couldn't bring myself to use the word "pray," even though I wanted a word like that, bigger than "hope" or "future."

AT OUR FIVE-YEAR college reunion that spring, I ran into a classmate who happened to be an oncology fellow at Northwestern. When I inserted Radhika's name into our conversation, he mentioned that he'd been involved in her diagnosis and care. "Best case scenario," he said, brimming with his secret, specialized knowledge, "she's got seven to ten years."

I KEPT TRACK of her for a while. She was an intern, then a second-year resident. In a photo on the Northwestern Ob-Gyn website, I could see the markings of her illness: hair cropped close to her hollowed temples; cheekbones like birds' wings. But I could also see the fire in her. Even in a blurry internet photo, it burned hotter than ever.

The following year there was a short *New York Times* wedding announcement:

Radhika Radhakrishna, 27, daughter of Harini and Prashanth Radhakrishna of La Grange, Illinois, will be married to Adam Chevalier, 28, son of Margaret and Richard Chevalier of Los Angeles, CA.

So, she had survived. At least for now. But I kept thinking of our classmate's grim prognosis. Seven to ten years.

After a while I stopped typing her name into my internet search field, too afraid I would find her obituary.

4

THE MAGAZINE ARRIVED on a Saturday. It happened to be my thirty-ninth birthday. I was making coffee, picking through the mail on the kitchen counter, when I paused on the latest issue of the *Atlantic,* its shiny cover beckoning from a pile of bills and municipal notices. The feature headline was "The Choice: An Abortion Doctor Faces Motherhood and Mortality." The author was Radhika Radhakrishna.

I flipped hungrily to the essay and read it straight through. Much of what it contained I already knew, or might have suspected: Radhika had always been ambivalent about becoming a mother, and a doctor, for that matter. As a second-generation Indian American, the daughter of two doctors, she'd felt these roles were expected of her, and she'd balked at slipping into them too easily. When she'd discovered a field of medicine she loved—not just obstetrics but abortion care specifically—she'd found not only the rewards of the work itself, which she described as "helping a woman to write the story of her life," but a unique chance to be a doctor in an "unexpected" role. "Our society tends broadly to valorize mothers and vilify abortion providers. But I reject those poles of judgment. I exist as both. I have written my own story."

The pregnancy in her last year of medical school had been an accident—she might have missed a pill or two while working her erratic hospital schedule—but it was a happy one. She and Adam had been talking about marriage; they both wanted children. They planned a wedding for the following year. They moved into an apartment with a spare room for a nursery.

Then came the diagnosis: a lump like a jagged pebble near her left armpit, the mammogram, a biopsy. She was twenty-six years old.

The doctors would cut out the tumor immediately, they assured her. But in order to avoid harm to the eight-week embryo, she would have to wait until the second trimester to undergo chemotherapy. Radiation therapy, too, would be delayed until after delivery.

She had an abortion within days of receiving the diagnosis.

"No one blinked at this," she wrote. "No one will blink now, reading it. You will feel for me. You will grieve for me. But you will not judge me. (At least, most readers of this magazine won't.) But plenty of people, no matter what they believe about abortion, will balk at what I did next."

No longer pregnant, she allowed the doctors to cut out the tumor, and the breast. She intended to undergo all their recommended treatments. But first she wanted a different cocktail of drugs. "Before they zapped my ovaries to oblivion, robbing me of any future chance at having my own family, I wanted them to induce ovulation and harvest my eggs for freezing. It seemed the least they could do."

The procedure was a success: combining her eggs with Adam's sperm, her IVF specialist was able to grow and freeze nine embryos. Afterward, while those embryos waited in their little plastic dishes, Radhika endured chemotherapy and radiation, including more than one harrowing complication that brought her close to death. But after all of it she not only survived, she surpassed her doctors' expectations. "Every prediction they gave me, I defied. Every limit, I shattered." She did not say precisely what those predictions were. I recalled that "seven-to-ten-year" figure and wondered if she had ever been given a number, if she had even wanted one. "It doesn't matter anymore," she wrote. "My life is no longer the kind based on predictions and statistics and chances. I've left all that behind. I have written my own version of the story."

After four years of residency and a two-year fellowship, her body showed not so much as a speck of cancer on all the fancy scans. Her doctors warned her of the risks. Her cancer was hormonally responsive, meaning that even a few tiny, malignant cells could respond aggressively to the high-estrogen state of pregnancy, spreading throughout her organs and once again threatening her life. Despite these warnings, she asked them to implant two of the frozen embryos, thinking she would be lucky if just one of them survived and grew. "This is what 'choice' means," she wrote:

Not just the choice to end a pregnancy, but the choice to begin one, even when everyone tells you it's not worth the risk. Whose body is it, after all? Whose life is it? Thankfully, my doctors understood this. They trusted me to make my own decision.

Now she was the mother of twins.

I tell this story not as proof of redemption or of some kind of "just world" fantasy, but as evidence of what I've always believed, and believe even more now: endings matter. Abortion allows a pregnant woman to be the author of her own life. Rather than living at the mercy of events that happen to her—biological, sexual, circumstantial—she can write the ending she wants. I can help shape the arc of the story to get her there.

Of course, she concluded, the decision of whether and when to have children must be a choice for all women. "But for me, even with all the attendant risk, it was the only choice."

THE DISCOVERY OF Radhika's essay upended my intentions for that morning: a walk on the beach, reading the hardcover novel I'd bought myself as a birthday gift. All my simple, solitary plans dissolved into the smudged pages of the magazine. I poured another cup of coffee, sat down at the counter, and read the essay again. Then I moved to the armchair by the window and read it a third time.

After a while I looked up, rubbing my eyes in the midday sun glinting off the ocean. In the distance, little black figures hurdled over the waves—surfers. I smoothed the magazine over the armrest beside me, thinking about Radhika and all that had happened to her, all the things I didn't know and might never know.

Through the open window a slice of cool air landed on my face. I looked up at the framed photograph above my desk, the only one I have of my parents and me. I used to look at that picture whenever I was feeling sorry for myself, or whenever my writing stalled—which was often in those days. I suppose I had, and still have, this idea of them watching over me, wondering if I would fulfill their hopes and expectations, wondering what, if anything, I would accomplish. What orphan doesn't think of her parents this way?

But that morning, for the first time, I saw something else in that picture. It was in the intention in their eyes, and the bridge of my dad's sinewy forearm between my mother and me. I understood that this was what Radhika was saying in her essay: Family doesn't just happen. Family was something you had to create; you had to take a risk for it—the way she had done, and my parents too, in a way. And I could take that risk, without anyone else's help. Instead of constantly trying to prove something to them, maybe there was something I could give—all the more meaningful because it was what they had given me, the same thing Radhika had given her children: a life.

5

"D ID I EVER mention my friend who got breast cancer right after college?"

It was the Monday after I'd been at Radhika's house. My friend Eleanor and I were sitting in a patch of sun on the northeast patio outside Davies Symphony Hall. I often timed my lunch to coincide with her short breaks in rehearsal. "The girl who died?" Eleanor asked, unwrapping her sandwich. "In medical school or something?"

"So I did tell you."

"Mm-hmm. More than once." This surprised me. Eleanor and I were close in the way I imagine blood relatives can be close. We looked out for each other. We didn't necessarily tell each other the most intimate details of our lives.

"Well, it turns out she didn't die. She's actually here in San Francisco."

"Wow. What happened to her cancer?"

"I guess they cured it after all? I don't know the details."

I spun some leftover pasta around a plastic fork. "I came across something she wrote. In the *Atlantic*."

"Ah. I see."

"It was really good. It was about her cancer, and motherhood. She has twins now."

"Does she? Good for her."

I heard the change in her voice, and I held myself back. I'd never asked Eleanor if she wanted children. She'd had a boyfriend for a while, a French Korean pianist whom she used to visit in Paris when she was traveling nine months out of the year with her quartet. Not long after she stopped touring, he met a French woman, got married and had a kid with her.

I sealed my empty Tupperware container and decided to follow a different thread. "You know how sometimes you feel jealous of someone you absolutely shouldn't be jealous of? Like, 'You were diagnosed with terminal cancer when you were twenty-six. How completely presumptuous and idiotic of me to think I would want to switch lives with you.'"

Eleanor looked at me quizzically. "I mean, would you ever want to switch lives with anyone? Look at Princess Diana. Or Luke Perry."

I laughed. "I didn't know you knew who Luke Perry was."

THE NEXT TIME I went to Radhika's house I let myself in through the back door, as she'd told me to. I came straight from the pool, wet hair, nipples stinging from the cold. That unshakable chill was my only symptom in those early weeks, my whole body like one giant goosebump.

Mercy was in the kitchen. "Oh. Hi." I had no reason to think she remembered me, even though we'd been introduced just a few days earlier at the Día de los Muertos party, where her handshake—smooth palms, calloused fingertips—had sent an electric charge up my arm. "I'm Josie. Is Radhika here?"

She smiled and stuck out her hand again. I noticed now, as I had before, a tiny "equal" sign inked on the inside of her wrist. "Mercy." Then she added as though reading my mind, "I remember you." She couldn't have been more than twenty-five. I blushed. She released my hand and continued moving around the house like it was her own, pulling things out of drawers, filling her water bottle, plugging her phone into the charger on the counter. "I'm just heading upstairs for bedtime. I'm sure Radhika will be down as soon as she can escape."

"Okay. Thanks." I couldn't figure out what to do with my hands, so I stuck them in my front pockets, where they rested over my tiny, invisible secret.

Radhika came downstairs and started making tea. I watched her, taking note of where everything was—mugs in the cupboard above the stove, tea tins in the opposite cabinet—so that the next time I could be helpful while I waited for her.

We sat side by side at the table. She turned her chair to face mine.

"I read your novel, Josie."

"The whole thing?"

"Everything you gave me." She touched my forearm. "I can't be the first person who's told you how good it is."

"You're the only person who's read it."

She blinked. "Well. That has to change." She smacked her palm on the stack of pages between us. "Are you ready?"

I nodded.

"Let's get to work."

With her red pen, she began marking up the very first paragraph, the first sentence. "You've got this great dystopian, Little Orphan Annie premise: the orphanage, these teenage girls competing for love and attention from the woman who runs the place and the people who come to visit. Competing to get adopted, basically. The tone and pacing are really excellent. It keeps getting darker and more sinister, and the tension keeps building as the main character—it's interesting she doesn't have a name, by the way—anyway, as this nameless main character grows more desperate. But she's not very good at playing the game, is she? And the harder she tries to compete, the deeper she digs herself into a hole."

"Right," I said. "Exactly. That's what I'm going for."

She nodded. "It's working. It's really good. Right up to the place where you've left off, where she's dug herself so deep it seems like she might never get out. Like she might be stuck there forever."

I bent my head, watching her red pen fly over the page. But my heart was floating above me, soaring. I'd spent years creating this world, these characters, particularly the main character, whom I cared so much about. And now someone was peering inside that world, seeing that character's desperation and her impossible dilemma. I'd created something decipherable, even emotionally complex and satisfying. A story.

I felt my whole body warm from the inside out with the promise of what was to come. My baby. My book.

I USED TO keep a diary in the years before my parents died. By the time I left to go live with my grandparents, I had rows and rows of cheap spiral notebooks lined up on the shelves beside my bed, each one filled with my neat handwriting. I didn't take them with me.

Other than the one framed photograph of me and my parents, I have only a cardboard box containing a couple of swim medals, a pink rabbit's foot keychain, a stiff placard of my own footprints from the day I was born—the kind of bland, sentimental keepsakes only a fourteen-year-old would hold onto.

My grandparents had the piano shipped to Toronto, where they installed it in the cold, depressing parlor with the dark wainscotting and latticed windows. But they never found a teacher for me. I guess they had other things on their minds, raising a teenage girl. And I didn't express a lot of interest. I would play around sometimes, aware of no one listening but the birds on the other side of the quivering glass. I would imagine my dad's murmured encouragements, my mother's astute criticism. *Try that again, Josephine.* The feeling of the keys under my fingers and my feet on the pedals only made me miss them more. Eventually I stopped playing altogether.

Several years later, after my grandparents died, I went through their things and was surprised that they, too, had kept few pictures or mementos of my parents. It was too late to ask them why. I suppose everyone has their own way of grieving, and remembering.

IN GRADUATE SCHOOL I moved into an apartment in the Outer Sunset, where I still live now: a 1920s rent-controlled walkup a few blocks from Ocean Beach, with a giant west-facing window. The living room, where I set up my small writing office, is dark and drafty in the mornings and stuffy and bright in the late afternoons, when the sun takes its sweet time sinking over the ocean.

On the wall over my desk, I hammered a nail and hung that one photograph of my parents and me. It was taken at the lake in the Sierras where we spent summer vacations, hiking and reading and swimming. It had hung in my dorm in college, and at my grandparents' house, and everywhere I've lived since.

I'm in my ragged blue one-piece, the elastic stretched at the neck and legs. My stance is, I think, typical of a fourteen-year-old girl, at once self-conscious and defiant, skinny legs planted, one arm pulled across my chest, chin turned up and to the side, as though I won't quite deign to look at the camera. Dark ponytail over a tanned shoulder. My dad is crouched beside me, and next to him sits my mother in shorts and a T-shirt, elbows wrapped around her knees, a book at her hip. They're both lean and muscled even in their fifties, their eyes crinkled with laughter. I have a more measured gaze: lips closed over a mouthful of braces, my eyes narrow, as though I can see what's coming.

DURING THOSE FIRST few years after college, something changed—about me, or about the writing, or both. Unlike Radhika, who always treated writing as an almost sacred privilege—*I'm jealous of you, truth be told*—my grad school classmates and I talked about writing primarily as a vocation. Instead of a solitary process, it became sort of a club that we belonged to. When they all dispersed after graduation, to New York or to undergraduate teaching positions at tiny Midwestern colleges, I remained in San Francisco, in that same apartment, writing at the same desk.

Sometimes sitting at that desk, or in the armchair facing the ocean, I caught glimpses of what the process had once been for me: those long, quiet weekends in the college library, scribbling my ideas onto the page. Tea bags scattered on the table like dead birds, the green glow of the table lamps in the darkening afternoon. Polishing my sentences until they shone like diamonds, my whole body thrumming with the certainty that I was creating something intelligent and crisp and original.

And what it had been for me even before that: the feeling of my hand moving across blank paper, too young to string words together but old enough to understand that marks on a page, lines and dots and loops, were what connected me to a larger world. A buttress against loneliness, a way of earning the attention and approval of others, of speaking when there's no one there to listen.

6

A T FIRST I kept asking Radhika to give me something of hers to read. She always said something like: "But I can't stop thinking about *your* novel. We can work on my stuff later." I assumed at some point we would fall into a natural rhythm, taking turns—a few weeks on the novel, then a few weeks on her book. But it didn't happen. The balance was so blatantly uneven, it began to worry me.

"Are you sure you're getting enough time to work on your own writing?" I asked her.

She assured me she had enough time. Monday through Thursday she worked in the abortion clinic at the hospital; Fridays she stayed home to write. Mercy took the kids to and from their preschool, entertained them in the afternoons, put them to bed in the evenings. Occasionally Rad worked a Saturday or evening shift on Labor & Delivery, but in general her weekends were her own. Adam took the kids on adventures—Giants games, the Exploratorium, Chinatown, trolley rides—while she holed up in her basement office. "It's enough time," she said. "I can't spend every minute of it alone, just writing. That can get boring. Even lonely."

I said, "Yeah. I know that problem."

"Ha. Not for long. Once this baby comes you'll be pining for those long, uninterrupted hours."

I bit my lip, thinking of another thing that had been worrying me. "And what about your kids? Are you getting enough time with them?"

"More than enough."

"I bet they can't get enough of you, though." I'd meant it as a compliment, but her face darkened. "I just mean they obviously adore you. You seem like a natural mother."

"I'm not a 'natural mother.'" Her air quotes were like bared fangs.

"Why do you say that?"

She seemed to compose herself for a moment. She poured a bit of mint tea, tasted it, then poured more into both cups. "Don't get me wrong. I love my kids. But I don't love *being* a mom."

She pushed a mug toward me. I wrapped my hands around it. "What's the difference?"

"Ah. Good question. It's pretty simple really. In a way you're right. The love comes naturally. I love my kids more than anything in the world. I would die for them." I watched the muscles of her jaw ripple against the bone. "But that love isn't synonymous with *being* a mother. It's not *unique* to being a mother."

I wasn't sure I agreed. I thought of my grandparents and the love they'd shown me. It was the deepest and truest love they had to give, undoubtedly. And still it had felt like a poor substitute.

"I'm very fortunate," she went on. "I've got the best nanny on the planet living in my house, and a partner who's a great, involved dad. Adam actually says there's nothing he'd rather do with his weekends. Which makes sense for someone who, you know, moves money around all day for a living." I looked down at the grain of the wooden table. "But the point is that he and Mercy are actually *better* at it than I am. I have no problem admitting that."

I could see her logic, and I admired her honesty. I tried to say something to that effect. "I guess the mothers in Victorian England did it that way, and no one said they weren't good mothers."

"Exactly!" I could see she had thought about this before. Her chest lifted and dropped in a sort of satisfied sigh. Then a long silence fell between us, during which I suppose we each drifted into our own thoughts. I was thinking of my mother and how I'd felt robbed of time with her—but only after she died. I was a quiet, bookish kid who was happy spending hours alone in my room, drawing and writing in my notebooks. Now I wondered: Had I been a different sort of kid, one who demanded more interactive play and entertainment, how would my parents have managed?

Radhika must have read my mind. In a different, softer tone she asked, "What do you remember about the time your mom spent with you?"

I thought for a moment, then said, "I don't really remember the time itself, how much or how little she spent with me." I hesitated, knowing better than to say, *I can tell you what I don't remember. I don't remember ever being left with a nanny. I don't remember anyone but her ever singing or reading me to sleep.* Instead I said: "I only remember what it felt like to be loved by her."

She nodded. "That's what I mean." Then she leaned in until our foreheads were practically touching, and she whispered, like she was sharing a secret: "You want to know something, Josie? There is nothing in the world I'd rather be doing than this. What we're doing right now. Nothing."

This made me feel lucky, and strangely sad. "You're good at knowing what you want," I said.

She leaned back, lifting her chin slightly. "Yeah, well. Facing your own mortality gives you some clarity."

I thought about this. I wondered whether a serious illness like cancer really changed a person, or just made them more like what they already were. I was remembering Radhika in college: Her raised hand. Her piercing, insightful criticism. *The author has to make a choice.* Tentatively, I said, "I read somewhere that confidence is the most important trait in a mother. That little kids and even infants can sense when their mom is sure of herself, and it makes them feel secure."

She said, "Mmmm, maybe." But a faraway look had come over her, and once again she was drifting in her own thoughts. I felt the hardness of the chair under my bony thighs, the edge of the table digging into my wrist.

"I guess it's something I'd better start working on," I said with a little laugh. I heard myself fishing for her reassurance and praise, and I hated myself for it.

But she didn't seem to notice. After a moment she lowered her chin and picked up her red pen, tapping it on the manuscript. "Where were we?"

7

EVERY WEEKDAY MORNING I walked from the bus stop at Civic Center through the grimy sidewalks of the Tenderloin and past City Hall, where couples of all combinations of gender, age, and race flocked the steps. Some wore traditional wedding gowns and tuxedos; others wore motorcycle gear, 49ers jerseys, scuba equipment. It was enough to remind you of the startling diversity of human life and love and celebration, and to make you feel—sometimes, anyway—that there was something wrong with you for never having ascended those steps yourself, fingers interlaced with another's, toward a future that felt infinitely more rich and hopeful than the foregone, lonely alternative.

The administrative offices on the top floor of Davies Symphony Hall had the same dated-but-regal ambience as the grand foyer, down to the pale pink bathroom tiles and art deco hanging lamps. Often during the workday I would head down a back stairwell to one of the rehearsal halls and find a seat in which to listen and take notes. Even pieces I knew by heart—especially those pieces—I wanted to hear again and again. It was a comfort: the *tap tap tap* of the conductor's baton, the pauses and patient repetitions, the same sliver of a melody making its slow, steady progress toward perfection. To me the sound of an orchestra tuning was, and still is, the most beautiful sound in the world.

After listening for a while I would often wander into the empty lobby and sit on one of the window benches with my notebook, pruning and rearranging words and sentences until they didn't merely describe the music but conjured it, like a remembered dream.

One afternoon in mid-November, as I was sitting there taking notes and humming a melody from a Shostakovich Piano Concerto, Radhika texted:

I've got news. See you tonight.

That evening at the dining table, she showed me an email on her phone:

Dear Radhika,

Thank you for sending me your friend's work, which I read with interest. I agree with you: the writing is superb. Understated and mesmerizing. And the story, or what she's written so far, is sharp and original. But (I'll risk stating the obvious): she needs to finish it. When she writes an ending, and if she's willing, I'd love to be the first to read it.

Talk soon,

Sarah

I shook my head, confused. "Who's Sarah?"

"Looks like you've got an agent." She grinned.

"But … Rad."

She laughed, maybe with a hint of impatience. "What?"

I swallowed. "I didn't ask you to send it to your agent."

"I know, I know." She waved a hand through the air. "I thought about discussing it with you first, but I knew what you'd say. And I honestly didn't know if she would even look at an unfinished manuscript. But I guess she was sold on your beautiful sentences."

Again, I asked, "Who is she?"

"Sarah Marshall."

I dropped my jaw. "Your agent is Sarah Marshall?"

"Have you heard of her?" The corners of her mouth twitched.

I lifted my hands to cover my face, but she grabbed my wrists. "Come on, Josie. Don't be a baby about this." She moved so that her eyes locked with mine. "Did you hear what she said? She wants to *represent* you. Come *on*."

For the first time, I felt so angry at Radhika I could've screamed at her. But I also felt big with excitement and self-importance. I imagined Sarah Marshall behind the high, reflective glass of the Marshall Agency, bent over my manuscript, a smile on her lips.

"But, Rad."

"What?"

I shook my head slowly. "I don't know how it ends."

For a moment she just looked at me, her eyes dull with impatience or pity. Then she leaned forward. "So do what Sarah Marshall said. Write the ending."

I REMEMBER ONLY a few conversations with my parents, although I've tried to recall more.

Thanksgiving Day. I would've been in the fifth grade. Some of their colleagues are coming for dinner, and the house is quiet with preparations. I've spent the morning reading *Little Women* for the first time. I wander to the kitchen, where my mother stands at the counter inefficiently stuffing a turkey, Mozart's A Major Clarinet Concerto playing on the stereo.

I tell her I've decided what I want to be when I grow up.

"Ah," she says. "A writer." Looking over her shoulder at me, the fingers of her right hand curled in their claw shape. "And what will you write?"

I rest my hip against the counter. "Books."

"What kind of books? Poetry? Scholarly criticism? A novel?"

I feel she is missing the point. "I don't know yet. Short stories, maybe."

She tilts her chin. "Have you ever read any short stories? In school or anything?"

As usual, she is making it all more complicated than it needs to be. "It doesn't matter, Mom. I like to write."

"But it's not enough just to like it. To be a writer, you have to write something."

"I write every day."

"In your diary. But that's not a story with a beginning, a middle, and an end. It's just writing whatever happens to you."

I rub my finger down a groove in the tiled counter. "Some writers publish their diaries."

Now she throws her head back and laughs. When she looks at me, her eyes are kind and serious. "Honey, but those are people who have done something, people the world recognizes as important. They're not ten-year-old girls." She turns away, sticking her partial fist back into the greasy bottom of the turkey. Between us the sad, soaring line of the clarinet rises and falls like a curtain.

THAT'S THE WORST thing about all those notebooks I didn't keep: all the details and moments, good or bad, that I could surely access if I had some word or image to jog my memory. I guess it didn't occur to my grandparents, or the other adults who helped pack up our house in Berkeley, that I might not be in a state of mind to make decisions like that: what to claim and what to leave behind. Probably they, like my mother, didn't think of a little girl's diaries as something worth keeping.

ANOTHER MEMORY, YEARS later, walking home after one of my very first college fiction workshops. It had been my turn to submit a story. As usual I'd written some thinly fictionalized account of my childhood and my parents—light on plot but dense with longing and pure, youthful certainty that some sense could be made of it all.

In the final moments of class, after listening while our classmates droned on about what "wasn't working" or what they "wanted to see more of," Radhika raised a languid arm in the air. The professor nodded at her. Under the table, I dug my fingernails into the insides of my elbows.

She said the story was well written but that it lacked "urgency." The questions being asked—*What if this? What if that?*—didn't matter to the reader without some more definitive action by the protagonist. "They're not *interesting* questions because they don't *lead* anywhere. They don't constitute a story with a beginning, a middle, and an end. Once this character starts making choices—that's when this will become a *story*."

The professor nodded along, as mesmerized as I was. Radhika tapped her pen a few times on her lower lip. I held my breath. Then she said, "I want to be clear that I think she's a very, very good writer. She could be … you know," she waved her pen through the air, "a *real* writer." The other students looked at the table or the ceiling. I saw one guy roll his eyes.

But I heard in her words a kind of music. It was the same music I'd heard as a girl, cross-legged on the floor of a university practice room with a pen and paper. I'm waiting for my father, who sits at the piano with one of his undergraduates. Feeling the chord progressions tremble through the floorboards into my bones: a lifting question, tension, resolution. An answer. Later, his student dismissed, my father crouches at my side to see how I've occupied myself, my sheet of staff paper covered in swirls and shapes and a few misspelled words, music notes scattered like birdseed in wild grass. A ruffle of my hair with his broad palm, his mustache tickling my ear. "You've got what it takes, Josephine Sampson. It's only a question of how you'll use it."

I left the workshop that night in a daze, my insides glowing like the edges of the fall sky. It was a feeling I would become familiar with, even a bit addicted to, as college went on: the feeling of being good at something and knowing it, and knowing others knew it. As I crossed the quad, tiny streams of cool air drifted over the grass and against my warm skin. Like a brisk, benevolent current, they seemed to lift me off my feet until I was floating.

$$8$$

EVEN AFTER EVERYTHING that's happened, I still remember those evenings fondly: the cups of tea between us on the table, the twins' art projects tacked on the walls. The sound of Radhika's voice, its steady thrum in the quiet house, the way it rose in pitch but not in volume when she wanted to make a particularly important point. We always sat on the same side of the table: me cross-legged in the chair, feet tucked under my thighs. Radhika's chair turned to face mine, her long toes curled over the edge of my seat, her bent knees forming a bridge between us.

The first night I came in bursting with ideas. "I think I've got to choose between one of two endings. I can make it all descend into chaos, *Lord of the Flies* style. The girls betray each other and the main character gets left behind in the orphanage, without any chance of getting out. Or I can write a happy ending, where the conflicts all get solved and the main character and the other girls all get out of the orphanage."

"Sure." Radhika looked like she had something to say, but she didn't say it. I rushed on.

"Or I suppose there's a third option, where some of the girls get out but some don't. Some of them get left behind. So there's sort of an ambiguous pathos to it."

I paused, waiting for her to speak, but she just blinked at me. "Or even that could go a few different ways, depending on which characters get left behind, and how the main character feels about it. I guess I could even play with what it means to be 'left behind' at all."

She breathed a little sigh and tapped her fingertips on the table. "Those are all possibilities."

I faltered. "Do you have another idea?"

Her mouth was a thin, stern line. "For an ending? No. That's for you to decide. It's got to come from you."

"But this is where I get stuck," I whined.

"I don't know what to tell you, Josie. You're going to get unstuck. You're *going* to write an ending."

For an instant I had the impulse to writhe and break free of this whole dumb idea, to return to my quiet apartment and keep tending to the book alone, as I'd been doing all along. "I've been trying to get unstuck for ten years," I muttered.

"Ah." Her smile was confident and serene. "But now you've got an agent. And a writing partner. And"—she pointed to my belly button—"a deadline." I must've looked surprised, because she said, "You want to finish by July, right? Before the baby?"

I nodded slowly.

She touched my arm. "You can absolutely do it, Josie. You just need to believe it."

So we went back to the beginning, rewriting every scene, every sentence. She made suggestions and I incorporated them. Then we reviewed the revisions together the next day. If Radhika wasn't satisfied, we discussed what was working or still needed improvement. Then I rewrote the scene again, and again, until finally she said, "Okay, I think this is fine, don't you? Let's keep going."

She never told me what to write or how to write it. She helped me see how to make the writing better. Her standards were higher than mine, and I strove to meet them. She gave me a kind of confidence and forward momentum I hadn't felt in years.

And still, privately, I agonized over an ending, because I knew that was what she wanted from me. Late at night and on weekends, alone in my apartment, I worked feverishly. I chose something, it didn't really matter what, and I wrote toward it. I really believed in it, like Radhika said. For a day, or even a few days. Then I would second-guess myself—*What if this? What if that?*—and stumble back, restarting, heading in a different direction.

I could see the absurdity of it: Something I'd been unable to do, applying myself diligently and sometimes despairingly for the past ten years, she now thought I was going to achieve in nine months. I could've told her it was impossible, even with her guidance and cheerleading.

It wasn't really her help with the book I wanted, then. It wasn't even her agent. Or it wasn't just those things. I was a motherless girl, angling for special attention from someone willing to give it. Someone to take me by the hand: "Here, I'll show you how to live your life." Which was exactly what Radhika did, or tried to do. That generous, appraising, instructive eye, the same one I'd known in college. Someone who could see past my facade of equanimity to the fierce, quiet ambition underneath.

Someone to whom I could prove myself, prove what I was capable of.

Also: I wanted her family. Everything about them. The warmth, the bustle, the big kitchen table, the Christmas tree and the stockings, the calendar on the wall marked with "First Day of School!" and "Last Day of Swim Lessons!" and "Holiday Concert!" I'd had it once, and I would have it again.

I wasn't naive; I knew I would have to give something in exchange. Like the sea witch who wants your voice, Radhika wanted something of mine—I suppose it was my stubborn self-reliance, the part of me that hated to ask for help, hers or anyone's. I was willing to sacrifice it for what she could offer me.

"HAVE YOU EVER heard of this event?" I held up my phone to show Eleanor the invitation. We were sitting at her kitchen counter, dipping chunks of cabbage and strips of pink beef into a bowl of steaming broth, on a rare weekday evening when she didn't have a rehearsal or a performance.

Eleanor peered at the screen. "No. But I know that organization. Who invited you?"

It was a holiday fundraiser for a Bay Area foundation that gave fellowships to "emerging women artists of color." Radhika and Adam were both on the board.

Eleanor peered at me. "Wait, this Radhika friend of yours—is she Radhika Radhakrishna?"

"You know her?"

"I know of her. Her husband is Adam Chevalier, right? They donate to the symphony and some of the museums. Patrons, I guess you could call them." I fished for a piece of drowned beef in the broth. I wasn't great at using chopsticks.

Eleanor said, "I think his family is, ah, extraordinarily wealthy."

I was remembering some of the links I'd scrolled over, scouring the internet for traces of Radhika. "I think his parents owned some art galleries at one point."

"Yeah. And I'm pretty sure she was board president of this foundation a few years ago. She has a lot of … influence, I guess you could say."

"That doesn't surprise me."

Eleanor raised her eyebrows. "Wow. And you guys are friends now."

"Not really friends," I said. "Just writing friends."

"She invited you to this thing, didn't she? Don't tell me she's expecting you to be a big donor."

"I hope not."

"And aren't you going to her place for Thanksgiving?"

It was true. The symphony was playing a special Thanksgiving Day concert this year, so I wouldn't have seen Eleanor anyway, but her brother Mark had invited me to join him for dinner at a friend's house. I'd spent Thanksgiving with Eleanor and Mark for as long as I'd known them. I'd had to tell him I already had plans.

Eleanor peered at me curiously. "I'm happy for you, Josie. You seem … I don't know, you've been kind of glowing lately."

I blushed and looked down.

"I think you really needed a writer friend."

"I guess I did."

I might've told her then. But Radhika had advised me to keep the pregnancy to myself during the first trimester: "I always tell my patients: only tell someone about the pregnancy if you'd be comfortable talking with them about a miscarriage."

I thought about Eleanor, childless by what I believed to be her own choice—a deliberate intention to focus on her mental health and her music career, to stop flying all over the world, bending over backwards for a boyfriend whom she may or may not have wanted to marry. She was happy in her focused, settled life. It seemed selfish to drag her into the saga of my own reproductive hopes and disappointments. If I had this baby, she would be happy for me. That was enough.

ON THANKSGIVING DAY, while Adam and Radhika cooked, I spent hours on their living room floor playing Uno with Sachin and Saniya. They warmed to me, and I found that I actually enjoyed their company: Sachin's silly humor, Saniya's fierce competitiveness. Mostly I was relieved to prove myself as someone more than just another adult who occupied their mother's time.

At dinner I took a few sips of the wine Adam poured for me, then covered the glass with my hand when he offered a refill. I'd half assumed Radhika had already told him about the pregnancy, but I quickly realized it was still our secret. He talked cheerfully about other things, asking me about my degree in fiction writing, my novel, books I was reading. I liked it this way, the sense of privacy and intimacy between Radhika and me. It was a feeling I imagined couples must share: *For now it's just ours. Nobody else needs to know.*

THE SUNNY FALL faded into short days and damp, cold nights. Then winter: the busy season at the symphony, wreaths on the lampposts around Opera Plaza, the flimsy hall radiator rattling away in the mornings while I wrote under a circle of lamplight.

It seems like an impossibly short time, those ten weeks between Halloween and Christmas when we created this ritual—this bond that seemed to be about writing but was, when I think of it now, about something else entirely. Whatever it was, whether its premise was real or imagined, I'm certain we felt it equally. We needed each other equally.

9

R ADHIKA'S HOME AS a Victorian novel: elegant surroundings, decorum, adult conversation, the children almost entirely offstage.

Always I was aware of Mercy in the house, my body attuned to her presence. But I hardly caught a glimpse of her. She knew her role and executed it faithfully, diligently. From the kitchen I could hear the kids upstairs, giggling through their bath, laughing and shrieking as Mercy hustled them off to bed. At first I would smile at these cheerful sounds and glance at Radhika, but she kept her head down. Eventually I learned to tune them out, too, and focus on the work at hand—a skill I figured I'd need as a mother.

Clearly the kids loved Mercy, though occasionally Saniya would stage a protest, escaping downstairs to snatch one last ounce of attention from her mother. "Mama, I want *you* to do bedtime. *Pleeeease*???"

"Saniya, you know that's not how it works." Radhika pushed a loose pile of construction paper to the end of the table, clearing a space for our laptops. "Please go upstairs and put on your pajamas."

"I'm already in my pajamas," Sachin declared from the doorway.

"Yes, Sachin. Thank you. Now Saniya—your turn. Mercy's waiting for you. Go."

"No! I hate Mercy! Why does Mercy always have to do bedtime so you can work?"

"You don't hate Mercy. You love Mercy. And you just answered your own question: she does bedtime so I can work."

"But you *always* work!"

"I'm not having this conversation, Saniya."

Then Mercy's brisk footsteps descending the living room stairs. Her voice, relaxed and cheerful, from just beyond the doorway: "Excuse me, did anyone else remember that we have a new *Bluey* book to read? But only for kids who are in pajamas, in bed, before I count to twenty. One ... two ... three ..."

Sachin dashed for the stairs.

Saniya let out a little grunt of frustration, trembled with indecision like a squirrel, then stomped after her brother. Then from upstairs, the click of the bedroom door, muffled laughter, Mercy's low, rhythmic reading voice. That was the last we saw of them for the night.

"Well, she handled that," I said, impressed.

Radhika said nothing, just tapped the edges of the pages I'd brought with me and placed them flat on the table. I could see her jaw clenching as she uncapped her red pen and began slowly turning the pages, looking over my work.

"I think it's admirable, you know," I said after a moment. "Your focus, your resolve. They might not understand it now. But one day they will."

From under her dark lashes, she flicked her eyes at me. "I hope you're right," she said. "I hope one day they'll understand."

10

THE NIGHT OF the fundraiser, Radhika answered the door wearing a kimono-sleeve black dress and ankle boots, her eyes lined in black, her lips a deep red. Long, gold earrings brushed the tops of her shoulders. "No coat? You must be freezing!" She ushered me into the hallway.

It was the Saturday before Christmas, and it was true, somehow I'd forgotten to put on a coat. I wore slacks, a black cardigan over a silk tank top, and ballet flats. I'd left the house feeling elegant, having swapped my glasses for contacts and a little makeup, dabbing perfume on my collarbones. But now, shivering after my bus ride, I felt small and childlike next to Radhika. Over her shoulder I could see Adam in the kitchen, tall and regal in his tux, spooning macaroni and cheese into the kids' bowls while they laughed over some four-year-old humor. I thought of the embryo inside me—a girl, I'd learned that morning, from the results of yet another blood test. Part of me felt sorry for her, this tiny being who had no one but me to carry her through the world.

I followed Radhika into the kitchen, where Sachin greeted me with his mouth full of macaroni. "Hi Auntie Josie!" Saniya climbed down from her stool and stood silently at her mother's elbow, fingering her long, silky sleeve, wrapping herself in the folds of her skirt. I, too, had a hard time taking my eyes off Radhika and Adam: the gold cuff bracelets around Radhika's delicate wrists, the angle of Adam's jaw over his collar, the way he touched her arm while she refilled his wineglass. I knew heads would turn when they walked into the fundraiser, these two physically perfect human beings. And I would walk alongside them.

Familiar footsteps coming up the basement steps, then, and there she was, with that fresh, healthy look of a college athlete after practice: Mercy. Dark, wet curls grazing the shoulders of her hoodie; small teeth; short fingernails; a shiny row of piercings running up the curve of one ear. She slid onto a stool between me and Saniya. She smelled of shampoo. I bit my lip.

Saniya immediately began picking up tiny shell-shaped noodles with her fingers and placing them in Mercy's open mouth. "Mmm, yum. Thanks."

"Saniya, I want you to eat at least *some* of your dinner," said Radhika. Then, turning to Mercy, "I have no idea when we'll be home. Is that okay?"

Mercy said of course, hardly seeming to hear her. She was licking her thumb between bites and rubbing at a streak of red marker on Saniya's forearm. I felt, as always, a twinge of envy at the casual intimacy—the private gears of a family turning, leaving me just on the outside. Over the past six weeks I'd spent nearly every weeknight in that kitchen, and still hardly a few words had passed between me and Mercy. She was always fully occupied, as she was tonight—the kids on either side of her, demanding her full attention. Now Radhika and Adam were gathering their things, and I was following them. Sachin and Saniya were yammering at Mercy about something or other. Radhika stopped at the door to the laundry room. She grabbed something off the counter: a plum-colored pashmina, so fine and soft it shimmered under the kitchen lights. She held it up, draped it over my shoulders, and arranged it around my bare throat. In the mirror by the door I glimpsed my reflection, how the shawl brought out the pink in my cheeks and lips. There was no doubt it made me look older, more sophisticated.

"There," said Radhika, looking over my shoulder. "Much better." Then, perhaps realizing I might take this as a criticism, she added, "You'll be warmer this way."

I smiled at her in the mirror, and she smiled back. Then she turned toward the door, which Adam held open, twirling his keys on one finger. Her heels clicked down the concrete stairs to the garage. I felt a strange, conflicted longing: to follow the two of them into the bright, brilliant evening, and also to stay behind in the warm house, to spin on a counter stool and eat macaroni and cheese out of a plastic bowl and curl under a blanket on the couch next to a kind, responsible babysitter.

WE DROVE EAST over the Bay Bridge, the lights of the city sparkling in the rearview mirror. Across the black water the shipping cranes loomed in the port of Oakland like ghosts.

Radhika glanced over her shoulder at me. "You warming up back there?" I pulled the shawl tighter around my throat and told her I was comfortable.

The event was at an enormous house in the Oakland Hills. Crystal chandeliers, coat service, servers circulating with trays of appetizers. The guests were surprisingly young and stylish—at least compared to the symphony crowd. I hovered close to Radhika and Adam while they greeted people by name. Radhika introduced me as a "dear friend" and "a writer." It was easy to identify the grant recipients, who were even younger than the other guests, and were among the very few brown and Black people in the room. Watching them smile graciously at the congratulations of others I felt the weary self-consciousness of what I was: a well-meaning bystander, blameless and superfluous, showing my support for a good cause without having to step out of my comfort zone or make any sacrifice. I hadn't even paid for my own ticket; I was there on Adam and Radhika's dime.

At one point I broke away and wandered to the massive window at the far end of the room, where a few other guests stood gazing out at the view: the clustered lights of San Francisco and Oakland, the parallel strands of the Bay Bridge, the glittering double peaks of the Golden Gate in the distance. All of it outlined by the flat, black water. It somehow reminded me of my first ultrasound photos, taken only a few weeks earlier. A whole world flattened into a black-and-white square that told the tea leaves of my future—the same future fluttering inside me now. The power and the terror of it washed over me, and I stepped back from the window.

A few days earlier, on a rare weekday when I hadn't been to Radhika's house—she'd been called in for an urgent procedure—I'd let that same fluttering terror get the better of me. It was a terror I'd felt off and on since the start of the pregnancy: the wonder of that tiny life mixed with a deep, wrenching fear of something else—the only word I knew for it was "death." Although I suspected it wasn't the right word, or the word Radhika would use. It was the fear of losing everything I'd started, of being empty again. Lying in bed, I'd known I wouldn't be able to sleep or breathe until I could be sure everything was okay.

It was after midnight when I called her. "I was just reading," she said, her voice alert. "What's up?"

I barely got the words out.

"I'll be right over."

She appeared twenty minutes later at my apartment door, fog clinging to her eyelashes and the sleeves of her fleece. She carried a handheld Doppler device and a canister of ultrasound gel. "Eleven weeks, right?"

I said that was right.

"We should be able to hear it. It helps that you're thin."

I lay on the couch and she smeared the gel under my belly button between my hip bones. Then with a firm, steady hand she pressed on the probe, angling her wrist back and forth in the darkness until it burst through: the thrum of a heartbeat, like horse hooves beating a gallop across the great distance between us. She'd found it.

She looked up and smiled. Then she shut off the machine, leaned over and brushed my bangs out of my eyes, wiping away a tear with her thumb. "So," she said, without a trace of *I-told-you-so* in her tone, "everything is fine."

I sniffed. "I'm sorry."

"For what?"

"For making you come all the way here."

She held up a palm like a wise, benevolent deity. "Stop. I get it. It's agony. Not being able to see it, not being able to control ..." She trailed off, and a faraway look came over her. Finally she said, "I did a lot of ultrasounds on myself, those first few months." In the dark living room, moonlight spilled through the window, shadowing the fine bones of her face. Then she turned and stared straight at me. "Don't think for a second—" She ran her tongue over her lips, took a breath. "Anyone who calls it a clump of cells—that's bullshit. They don't know what they're talking about." She looked as though she was daring me to challenge her. I wouldn't have dreamed of it. "That's your baby in there," she practically hissed. "Don't let anyone tell you otherwise."

COCKTAILS ENDED AND we were asked to move to the dining room. At Radhika and Adam's crowded table, I was seated under a vent that blew cold air down my back. Between stabbing bites of salad and trying to make pleasant conversation, I tugged Radhika's shawl tighter around my throat. A plate of salmon arrived; I finished it in a few bites. At a microphone in the front of the room, a woman started talking about the fellowship and all the talented young artists in our midst. I could hear my own teeth chattering. Radhika leaned over to me. "Hey. You okay?"

I said, "Just really cold."

"Poor thing. You're shivering. Do you want to find somewhere to lie down? I could ask if there's a guest room."

Feeling like a child, I said, "Actually Rad, I'm sorry, but do you think I could take a car back to the city? I just … I don't feel that well."

"Of course." She scanned me with her eyes, touched my forehead. I could see she was trying to work out whether something was really wrong. "Take your temperature when you get home. If you have a fever, take a thousand milligrams of Tylenol."

In the back seat of the car, I felt my body begin to thaw. "Thanks for having the heat on," I said to the driver.

He laughed. His voice was friendly and he had a heavy accent. "I always have it on. Driving is a cold job."

I let my eyes roam around the inside of his car while he talked on the phone with a tired-sounding woman in a language I didn't recognize, children laughing and shouting in the background. While we were crossing the bridge, I fished in my bag for my keys and realized I'd left them at Radhika's house. "Sorry, I'll have to give you a different address."

He said no problem, and punched Radhika's address into his phone. When we pulled up in front of the house, windows glowing, Japanese maples flanking the porch like sentries, I thought how different it was from the rusted gate of my apartment building. Instead of asking him to wait while I ran in for my keys, I acted as though this were my final destination. I guess I wanted him to believe it was.

I FOUND THE front door unlocked, the house quiet. Mercy was stretched on a couch in the living room, a paperback on her knees.

"Sorry," I said, "I hope I didn't startle you."

She looked up, unfazed. "No worries. Everything okay?"

"Yes. Fine. I left a little early, I wasn't feeling well. I think I left my keys here."

She gave a little smile and waved her hand through the air, like, *Make yourself at home,* then returned to her book. I wandered into the kitchen and found the keys on the counter, where they'd been shoved into a corner with a pile of other family paraphernalia: checkbooks, chargers, a frequent customer card for a drive-through car wash. I held them in my hand for a moment, heavy and comforting, then dropped them in my purse. When I turned around, Mercy was in the doorway, paperback curled in her palm. Even in the dim kitchen she cast a rosy glow.

"So how was it?"

"The benefit? Fine. I was really cold, for some reason. But the organization seems cool. They give fellowships to women artists. I guess Radhika's on the board."

"Yeah," she said. "I know all about it."

"Are you on the board, too?"

She laughed. "I was a fellow. A few years ago. When Radhika and Adam first moved here, and I was babysitting but hadn't moved in full-time. Radhika knew I was a musician, so."

"Ah, I see," I said, although I didn't quite get it. "What do you play?"

"The cello."

"Oh! My friend is a cellist—well, my friend's brother, actually. And she's a violinist. In the symphony. Mark and Eleanor Choi?"

"Hmm." This didn't interest her as much as I'd hoped. Her eyes never left mine, but they seemed to be searching for something more than my small talk.

"Where do you, ah, play?" I said.

"I don't anymore, I mean not in any formal way. This is my thing, now."

"You must've been pretty good if you got one of those fellowships. Why did you stop?"

She took a few steps into the kitchen and leaned her lithe, compact body against the counter. She had taken off her hoodie. Under her T-shirt her breasts were tight and round. "The question is why I got that fellowship in the first place. I think it had more to do with Radhika than with me."

"Oh, I'm sure that's not true."

She shrugged. "I studied music in college. But I never had any intention of doing it professionally. I'm not that … ambitious. Or at least I didn't live up to the ambitions of the fellowship committee. I applied to grad school in music performance and made some half-hearted audition attempts. Then as soon as the fellowship year was over, I dropped all of it. Rad offered me the live-in job. I just play for myself, now."

Once again I thought how young she looked. "And you're, what, twenty-six?"

She raised her eyebrows. "Yeah. Lucky guess."

"I think Radhika mentioned it."

There was a long pause, and I felt myself burn with something like desperation. I couldn't think of anything else to say to her, even though I wanted to. I opened my mouth to suggest that I should get going, when she said, "Are you still cold? Do you want some tea?"

"Sure," I said, too quickly. "I'd love some." She went to a cabinet and took out two mugs. She knew where everything was. "It's your home," I murmured, so quietly I thought she might not have heard.

She looked straight at me. "In a way it is. I'm moving out this summer, though. Once Radhika finishes her book and the twins start kindergarten."

"And then?"

"On to the next nannying job I guess." She filled the kettle with water. "What about you? What do you do for work?"

I told her about my job producing web and print copy for the symphony. "I get to listen to music and write about it. It's pretty great."

"You're a writer, then?"

I usually hated this question, but I found myself trying to answer it for her. "Kind of. I published a short story collection a long time ago."

"Oh! Jeez. You wrote a book."

"A very small book. I mean it didn't get much … It wasn't a big deal. I've been working on a novel for years, but—"

"But what?" She came over with two cups of hot water and a box of tea bags. We sat across the table from each other and she looked at me, waiting for an answer. In a long, strange moment I realized what gave her face that magnetic pull: her eyes. The lashes were so fine and short, they were almost nonexistent—spare, dark wisps that curled away from brown, nearly translucent lids. This gave her gaze a quality of open attentiveness, as though there were no barriers between her and the rest of the world. What you saw of her, and what she could see of you, was unfiltered. Pure.

"I'm having a hard time writing the ending. Radhika's been helping me."

"Ah. So that's what you guys do down here every night."

I nodded. "But you know what you said about not being that ambitious? I guess I relate to that."

We twirled our tea bags in our mugs. The steam turned the palms of her hands a dewy pink. "So," she said, "you've published a book of short stories and you're about to finish a novel." She squeezed out her tea bag and plopped it on a small dish between us. "Sounds like you're a real writer to me." It was the kind of remark that could've felt patronizing coming from someone else. But from her it felt like genuine admiration, even awe. I looked at her, then down at my tea. "Can I ask how old *you* are?" she said.

"Thirty-nine." I wondered what this would mean to her. *Nearly old enough to be your mother. Depressingly old.* But all she said was: "Same as Radhika."

"We were classmates in college. Friends, kind of. Actually, she helped me out when I needed an abortion." She seemed to regard this information the way I did: as a practical fact about my past that had little bearing on the present, other than whatever it meant about us, and what might be happening between us. "It's funny," I said, "I think that's why we have this sort of bond. Now she's helping me with the book. And with something else that's similar, but different. I'm pregnant."

Her eyes unpeeled, sweet and open. Her face erupted in a smile. "Wow! Really? Congratulations! That's wonderful."

For the first time since I'd peed on a stick in Radhika's bathroom, I felt the thrill and the warmth of another person's excitement for me, like sunlight on my skin.

"When are you due?"

"July." Hearing myself say it out loud, on a cold December night, it suddenly sounded very far away. "It's still early, obviously. No one else knows. Just Radhika."

"And your partner, presumably?"

I tried to keep my voice casual. "There's no partner. It's just me and this little bean." I placed a hand over my navel. I could feel my pulse throbbing in my palm.

"Wow. Good for you." She sounded genuinely impressed. "But also: you've got to be at least a little ambitious to go and make a whole baby all by yourself. Just saying."

I laughed. "Maybe a little. If you can call it an ambition."

"I think you absolutely can. That's basically what I figured out during my fellowship year."

"What, exactly?"

She looked at me with the bright, self-certain gaze of a young person just starting to find her own path, with all the excitement and promise that holds. "That I don't want to build my life around music and performance. I want to build it around family. Around needing others, and being needed."

I looked at my empty tea mug, then straight into her eyes. "It sounds pretty good, doesn't it?"

Her phone buzzed on the table. "It's Rad. They're on their way home."

"I should go," I said, and pulled out my phone to check for the next bus.

"Why don't you wait until they get back? I can drive you home. You must be tired."

I told her it was fine, I always took the bus. She didn't insist. But when we hugged at the door, she held on to me for a beat longer than I expected. I could smell her deodorant, the slight saltiness of her skin, whatever drugstore product tamed those tight curls. Our breastbones pressed together, and I felt her take a long, deep breath, as though she were smelling me, too. "I'm excited for you," she said as she pulled away, holding onto my elbows, looking at me intently. "And I want to—"

"Come over," I said. "You should come over. After she's born."

She smiled hesitantly at me.

"I mean, when you have more time. To, ah, babysit." I swallowed, meeting her eyes. "In July, right?"

"Yes." She smiled again, more broadly this time. "July."

ON THE BUS, I tapped my finger on the gray rubber at the base of the window and stared at the passing streets, feeling the ambient energy of a large, wheezing vehicle making its way through the city. At some point I realized I was still wearing Radhika's shawl. I wrapped it around myself and burrowed into the seat.

At home I stepped out of my shoes, peeled off my clothes, and lay face down on the bed. Reaching under the hem of my underwear, I rubbed my thumb in slow circles until I felt that unmistakable, unstoppable build, then breathless release. It took less than a minute. I lay there breathing into the sheets, my body limp, my baby safe inside me. I felt satisfied and complete.

11

THE FOLLOWING MONDAY after work, I waited for Eleanor in the musician parking lot, when I knew she would be arriving for rehearsal. "Can I ask you something?" I fiddled with the strap on my swim bag. "Would you mind terribly if I didn't come to Christmas this year?" Eleanor, Mark and I had a tradition of watching K-dramas and making hand-rolled sushi at Mark's house. It wasn't something they had to invite me to; I was just included, like another sibling. Eleanor had said to me once, "Don't take this the wrong way, but if you weren't gay, I would absolutely try to set you up with Mark." I was 99 percent sure Mark was also queer, though neither of them had ever said it out loud. In this way, too, they treated me like family.

She leaned against her car, cradling her violin case next to her hip. "Of course it's okay, Josie. Where will you be?"

"Radhika invited me." It felt strange saying this to her, especially because I wasn't sure it was entirely true. Radhika had mentioned it at Thanksgiving, but I hadn't asked her about a specific plan. It hadn't come up since, even though I'd seen her nearly every day. It seemed impossible that she would forget.

Now I watched Eleanor's face closely. "Maybe we could hang out on Boxing Day," I said. "Go to a museum or something."

She laughed. "How Canadian of you." But her voice betrayed no hint of jealousy or disappointment. "Are the museums open on Boxing Day?"

AFTER THAT I didn't see Radhika all week. The schools were closed for winter break; the twins were at home. Mercy had the week off and was staying at Myra's house. "It's kind of a zoo around here," Radhika texted me. "Not exactly a place where you can think in complete sentences." She didn't mention plans for Christmas.

I kept busy with my old routine: swimming, riding the bus home, writing and reading in the armchair. Outside the CVS on the corner, a Salvation Army man stood with his red bucket. In the rare moment when no bus was going by and the jackhammers were silent, I could faintly hear his ringing bell.

I tried to write, but when I wasn't worrying about whether Radhika would call, I was distracted by a new, exciting thrum that pulsed underneath everything: Mercy.

I thought about her while I was swimming laps, editing holiday symphony programs at work, addressing Christmas cards to old classmates and friends who'd moved away. I tried to keep up with things like that.

I wondered if Mercy had said anything about me to Radhika. Of course not. What was there to say? Our conversation had felt intimate and important to me, but to her it had probably been just another night at Radhika and Adam's house, a chat with their nearly forty-year-old pregnant friend who offered unsolicited advice about how to be a failed artist.

But. The way she'd held on to me by the door. The way we'd both hinted at seeing each other again. Every time I thought about her my insides throbbed until I could barely walk. The whole thing was at once intensely exciting and, if I thought about it too much, embarrassing. She was thirteen years younger than me, just a few years out of college. Radhika talked about her—not like a child, exactly, but like a younger sister. Someone not quite formed.

BY FRIDAY AFTERNOON, Christmas Eve, I was the only person left in the symphony offices. I took an early lunch and walked over to the bookstore in Opera Plaza, looking for a Christmas present for Radhika. I eventually selected a poetry collection by an ICU doctor that I'd heard hyped on one of my literary podcasts. Then I picked out some coloring books for Sachin and Saniya. The woman at the register offered to gift wrap all of them, but I wanted to wrap them myself, to hand a gift to Radhika that was understated, tasteful, personal.

Eleanor and I met for lunch in the courtyard next to the opera house, bundled in our fleeces and scarves. Mottled strips of fog, like wet flour, covered the sky. Dry leaves rustled in the gutters. Eleanor nodded at my shopping bag. "Last-minute gifts?"

"As usual."

She and I had stopped exchanging presents years ago. *I don't need you to give me a scented candle or a throw blanket to prove you love me,* was her approach to the holiday season.

Now I was thinking about asking if I could join her and Mark for Christmas after all. *Things are pretty hectic at Radhika's house. They might not be doing any formal Christmas thing, after all.*

But before I could think how to bring it up, Eleanor told me she and Mark were flying to Spokane that evening to spend Christmas with their cousin. "We really should go up there more. He's our only family in the US"

"Great!" I said, too enthusiastically. The wind from the empty city streets whipped around us, blowing Eleanor's hair into her tuna sandwich, carrying away my empty plastic bag. I reached into my purse for Radhika's shawl and wrapped it around my shoulders. "And good for you, El. Non-required airline travel. Wow."

Eleanor and I had met when we were both in our twenties. I was spending a summer on a writing fellowship in Europe and went to hear a renowned American string quartet play in Berlin. An hour after the concert, in a touristy café in Potsdamer Platz, the quartet's first violinist sat down at the table next to me, placed her violin case in the chair between us, and proceeded to disinfect every surrounding surface with a packet of Clorox wipes. She saw my book bag with the name of my graduate program in San Francisco, and struck up a conversation. She was easy to talk to, forthright but not overbearing. You could tell how much she loved her job, and how proud she was of it, in a quiet way. "But," she confided, "flying on an airplane more than half the days of the year with a deadly fear of airborne viruses— it's not sustainable. I should be at home, sleeping in my own bed, spending more time with my brother." She and Mark had left home when they were teenagers, when their parents sent them to the US from South Korea to study music.

"If I can play my cards right," she told me that evening in Berlin, "I'll quit the string quartet and wedge my way into a concertmaster position with the San Francisco Symphony."

And she did it. Not long after that, Eleanor, five-foot-one, with her straight bangs and serious eyes and her Clorox wipes, navigated the fiercely competitive and political world of classical music and got herself into the first chair of the San Francisco Symphony violin section. She was the one who helped me get my foot in the door of the editorial department not long afterward. And she'd been back in San Francisco ever since—sleeping in her apartment, touring only occasionally with the orchestra. Her OCD had improved dramatically.

She chewed her sandwich now, pushing strands of long black hair from the corner of her mouth. "Spokane is a short flight, at least. I'm planning on taking, like, half a bottle of Xanax before I even get on the plane."

I DECIDED TO skip my swim and took the bus home after lunch. It was midafternoon when I unlocked the door to my cold, dark apartment. I couldn't bear the thought of sitting there alone, the pathetic wall heater rattling in the corridor. I changed into sneakers and sweatpants, wrapped Radhika's shawl around my throat and set out for the beach.

Along Great Highway, a fierce wind gusted in off the ocean. Sand dunes piled along the pavement. As I often did when dreading a long evening alone, I made a plan for exactly how I would pass the hours: walk until dark, return home and take a bath, eat some dinner. I had those presents to wrap, a few more cards to write. The thought crossed my mind that by next Christmas, I would have my baby with me. But the comfort in this quickly dissipated. I remembered the warm, festive gatherings at my parents' house when I was growing up, the way they'd brought friends and colleagues into our home to make up for their otherwise faraway or nonexistent families. How merry and intimate it all felt: my father playing Christmas carols, his hatched tumbler of whiskey beside him on the piano. The adults singing boisterously, drinks and lyric books in hand. The other children following me around—how happy I was to show them my carefully tidied room, to watch *How the Grinch Stole Christmas* and *Home Alone* on the couch in the den while the adults sang and talked late into the evening. Then after everyone left, the feeling of my mom's muscled arms under my bottom as she carried me to bed, limp-limbed and happy.

How different to be a mom and a baby, just the two of us. I thought of my daughter growing up the way I had the other 364 days of the year, without siblings or other children around; and later, after my parents' death, in my grandparents' permanently hushed home in Toronto.

Another thought bubbled up in me, then, as it had a hundred times: what would happen to this baby, my daughter, if I wasn't around to take care of her? If I died, the way my parents had, when she was still young? Who would be her family?

My mind skimmed over the possibilities once again. Eleanor in her small, spotless apartment, with her grueling practice and performance schedule. An elderly aunt in Canada whom I hadn't seen in years. A shiver passed through me. I tugged the shawl tighter around my throat.

Then, I couldn't help it, I thought of Radhika and Adam, their young children, their warm and inviting home. I shook the thought away, but it kept forcing itself back in. Their proximity, their solidity and generosity. It wasn't such a crazy idea. Radhika and I might have only reconnected a few months ago, but we'd known each other nearly half our lives. If I asked her, what would she say? I fingered the braided fringe of the shawl as I walked, the grainy wind stinging my cheeks.

Deep in my fleece pocket, my phone buzzed. It was Radhika. I softened my shoulders down my back, modulated my voice to sound relaxed and casual. "Rad?"

"Josie. Hey, gosh, sorry this week has been nuts. Listen, are we still on for Christmas dinner tomorrow?"

The signal was choppy. I hunched my back to the wind to protect our connection, cupping my hand over the phone as though it were an injured bird. "Yes," I said. "We're on. I mean, I'm planning on it."

"Okay. Good." She sounded distracted. In the background, the kids shouted. "And no need to bring anything. It'll be low-key, just turkey or something. The kids want to make gingerbread cookies. Come over anytime, okay? We'll be here."

12

O N CHRISTMAS DAY the bus ran on a modified schedule, so I walked the last mile to Radhika's house through the cold, clear dusk, still wrapped in her shawl. My deep chill had returned, and by the time I slipped through the side gate my teeth were chattering, the tips of my fingers white.

I found Adam and the kids in the backyard, playing with a new bubble machine. The sun sinking behind the high fence threw a triangle of shadow across the porch. Adam told me Radhika had gone out for a run. Sachin called, "Josie, come play with us!" But I said I would stay inside if that was okay. "Of course," Adam said. "She'll be back soon. Make yourself at home."

I stood at the stove to boil water for tea, warming my hands over the gas range, scooping leaves from one of the pretty tea tins. Helping myself the way Mercy did.

In the living room, the carpet was strewn with the detritus of Christmas morning: torn wrapping paper, empty boxes, an etiolated, half-eaten candy cane stuck to the coffee table. The Christmas tree lights were switched off, the branches brittle and dark. I stretched out on the couch, the warm mug in my hands. After a few minutes I put the mug on the table and closed my eyes. I was remembering the days after Christmas in my parents' house, which had always felt a little sad. My dad used to listen to Chopin on the stereo while he took down the lights and the tree, the subdued, yearning melodies so different from the relentless cheer of Christmas carols. I remembered the look on his face, how he would draw his eyebrows together in concentration—or maybe it was sadness, his own sense of an inevitable ending.

Lying on Radhika's couch now, gazing at the dark tree, that sadness returned to me in all its childish, aching intensity. I rested my hands on my belly and thought of the tiny being growing inside me who would have her own sad days and nights, her own endings and disappointments. Her own pains, big and small, from which I could not protect her.

WHEN I AWOKE the sky had turned dark. I reached for my tea. It was cold. Someone had switched on the lights on the tree, making the whole room cozy and bright. Through the glass doors to the kitchen I could hear muffled shouts and laughter, Radhika's firm, calm voice speaking to the children, dishes under running water. I looked at my watch. Eight-thirty. I had missed dinner. The kids would be already on their way to bed.

"I saved you a plate," Radhika said when I emerged, squinting, into the bright kitchen. My eyes roamed over the table: scattered cloth napkins, half-empty glasses, red beeswax candles looped with pine branches. The twins, in matching candy cane pajamas, kissed us goodnight before following Adam upstairs.

"You must think I'm the rudest person ever," I said. "Leaving the fundraiser, falling asleep on your couch, missing Christmas dinner. When you were so nice to include me in all of it."

"Stop. You're pregnant and exhausted. You've got to sleep when you can. And I should've known better than to drag you to that fundraiser." She wrinkled her pretty eyebrows. "Have I really not seen you since then?"

"Oh! Dammit." I balled my hands into fists. "And I forgot the presents."

She batted a hand at me. "You think those kids need more presents?"

"But I had something for you. A book."

"Bring it next time."

It was the best thing she could have said, the only thing I wanted to hear: there would be a next time, and a next. I didn't care that she didn't mention a gift for me. It was like Eleanor said: *I don't need you to prove that you love me.*

Radhika heated a plate of leftovers and sat with me while I ate: curried cauliflower, roasted duck, Brussels sprouts. "You cooked all this?"

"Adam."

After the hot food she piled my plate with frisée, pecans, and pomegranate seeds. I found myself wondering what Radhika had been doing while Adam cooked Christmas dinner and played with their kids, how many hours she'd spent writing, alone in her office, before slipping out for her late-afternoon jog. Then I scolded myself. It didn't matter.

When I finished eating she said, "Stay for a while?"

I SAT ON the living room floor, leaning against the side of the couch. Radhika built an efficient fire in the fireplace, then sat cross-legged on the rug, reaching around her with her long arms like a spider, stuffing wrapping paper into a giant garbage bag in her lap. I was struck again by the coziness of the room: the dark windows, the bright lights on the tree. And yet I sensed, too, a certain emptiness. I thought about how the house felt with Mercy in it: at the Día de los Muertos party; nights when she giggled with the twins on the way to bed; her wide, bright eyes peering into mine, talking about pregnancy and family and ambition. In the quiet containment of the house that night, I felt her absence like a phantom limb.

Radhika was asking me about my progress on the novel over the past week. I told her vaguely that I'd been working on it. I tried to think of a way to ask her about Mercy, to tell her about our conversation at her kitchen table, which was starting to feel like a secret I was keeping from her. But I couldn't bring myself to say it.

Eventually she took the garbage bag to the kitchen and returned with a plate of cookies and two glasses of milk. We sat on the couch like bookends, our legs stretched out between us. I noticed a tiredness in her eyes.

"Do you ever get the post-Christmas blues?"

She gave me a weary smile. "Maybe that's it." She picked up a cookie and broke off one frosted gingerbread limb, managing the crumbs neatly, touching her fingertips to her tongue. "Maybe I've got the post-Christmas blues." Something about her seemed almost fragile. Her narrow feet in their wool socks, her brown ankles flecked with fine dark hairs. I thought of her cancer and a shudder passed through me. Every holiday and ritual must be bittersweet for her, tinged with the knowledge that it might never have been. I thought of telling her about my own childhood Christmases: the Chopin on the stereo, my dad's ritualized concentration, the quiet house. Instead I just said, "Don't worry. It happens to the best of us."

She tilted her head back and made a little sound of frustration, a sort of growl. "Honestly, I think I'm just ready for winter break to be over. Today was a lot of sitting around. Watching the kids play with their new toys. They didn't really *need* me there. I knew that. But I also knew it wasn't the right time to go off and write. I forced myself to just sit here. I mean it's Christmas, you know?"

So that's what she'd been doing while Adam cooked. I imagined the long afternoon: the mounds of wrapping paper, the smell of roasting vegetables, her two beautiful children playing at her feet. *Mama look! Mama, see what this does?* I didn't feel sorry for her. "Maybe that's what being a mom is sometimes. Just being bored." In the next breath, I added, "Not that I would know from experience, obviously."

She made a face. "No, you're absolutely right."

A log in the fireplace popped and hissed. Adam appeared at the foot of the stairs and blew a kiss toward Radhika. She blew a kiss back, then faced me again on the couch. She informed me that I would be spending the night.

"As long as it's no trouble," I said. There was nothing I wanted more than to sleep inside the warm walls of Radhika's house on Christmas, to wake up there the next morning, eat breakfast in her kitchen.

"Are you kidding? There's no way you're riding three different buses home on Christmas. You can stay in the guest room downstairs."

"Mercy's room?"

She frowned. "When Mercy leaves it'll be the guest room again. Tonight, it's your room. And sleep in—even though we'll be up early. Did I tell you we're driving to LA tomorrow?"

My heart sank. "You didn't mention it." I was thinking of another week going by without being in this house. The wrapped presents I'd left on the table by my front door. Next time.

"To visit Adam's parents for a week. And I'm already dreading it. They're great with the kids, they'll be a huge help. But it's still another whole week of this. No real time and space to write, no patients to see, nothing to really *do*." Her face pinched with distaste. "Although I guess we'll be making the requisite trip to Disneyland."

"Torture."

She winced. "I know. I'm a terrible mom."

"That's not what I meant."

And it wasn't. Even if I didn't feel sorry for her, I was beginning to see a side of her I hadn't known, in which she had her confident ambitions, and also her doubts and vulnerabilities.

Wanting to change the subject, I leaned toward the tree and touched an ornament that caught my eye, nudging it so that it spun on its red ribbon to face us. It was a silver picture frame holding a photo of two newborn infants, side by side in clear plastic bassinets. One baby was pink and strong, mouth wide open, fists pumping. The other was gray and tiny, strapped to tubes and monitors, eyes bandaged, belly taut. Scrawny, reptilian limbs. "The twins?"

She made a face. "What a gross picture to put on a Christmas ornament, right? My mom gave it to us."

I leaned closer to the photo, pointing to the smaller, sickly-looking baby. "Saniya?"

"No," she said. "That's Sachin."

I squinted at it. "That's Sachin?"

"Mm-hmm. He was the runt. Saniya just spent a few days in the NICU and then she was fine. Sachin was in there for almost three months, and he was … For a while there it seemed like he might not make it."

"Gosh," I whispered. Then I said, "You didn't write about that in the *Atlantic* essay."

She shook her head tightly, her face drawn and closed.

"I guess it's hard to write about."

"It's hard even to think about."

I looked at her for a moment, then at the picture, running my thumb over the cheap plastic frame. Then I leaned back on the couch. The feeling of dread from the day before—the thought of my own mortality—reared up in me, and I decided to ask Radhika my horrible question, that unspeakable yet necessary request. In case something should happen to me, in case my daughter should need another mother. Something about the quiet intimacy of that night, the sense of us being both totally alone and yet ensconced in the warm orb of her family home, felt like the best chance I would get. I opened my mouth, but then hesitated. Her eyes were still on the ornament swaying on its ribbon, locking her in the pain of her own experience. Something, the tender purity of the moment, had escaped. I let it go.

We talked a bit longer about nothing of consequence— the kind of banter I knew Radhika didn't have the patience for. Not long after that, before the last log had shriveled to its crispy shell, she yawned loudly and got up to find me a toothbrush and a pair of pajamas.

In the downstairs guest room, a few framed pictures of Sachin, Saniya, and Mercy's nieces stood on the dresser. A music stand and chair occupied a humble corner. The duvet was plump and heavy, the sheets as clean and white as snow.

THE NEXT MORNING I sat with Sachin and Saniya in the kitchen, feeling slightly ridiculous in a pair of their mom's pajamas, while Adam gathered up phone chargers, snacks, keys, coats, and Radhika drank a cup of coffee, thumbing through texts on her phone. And just like that, they were ready to go. "Hang out as long as you want, Josie," Radhika said as she rinsed her mug in the sink. "And lock the door, but no need to set the alarm. Mercy will be here sometime today anyway, to house-sit."

"Sure, no problem." I followed them down the steps to the garage. "I'll just get dressed and get going. I've got a busy day."

"Bye, Auntie Josie!" Sachin and Saniya called as the car pulled away. The garage door trundled shut behind them, swallowing me into the empty house.

I sat at the counter, sipping my cold coffee. A plan began to take shape in my head. Radhika's clean mug dripped in the dish rack. The smell of her perfume lingered in the air. Realizing I may not have much time, I stood, dumped the rest of my coffee in the sink and hurried downstairs to Mercy's room, where I stripped the bed and threw the sheets in the wash. Dashing out the side door, then, I hurried the two blocks to Safeway—open on Boxing Day, apparently— returning with a potted poinsettia and a single grocery bag stuffed with as much as I could carry: mushrooms, heavy cream, lasagna noodles, two bunches of kale. All of this I placed in the large fridge in the kitchen. I shoved the clean sheets into the dryer on high, waited impatiently for half an hour, then smoothed them back onto the bed, only the tiniest bit damp. The poinsettia went on top of the dresser, its velvety leaves wrinkled but still pretty.

Before returning upstairs I decided to peek into Radhika's office, just to glimpse the place where she did her real, solitary work. I took the door handle in my palm, but it wouldn't turn. I wondered if she always kept it locked, or only when she was leaving the house in someone else's care.

Within minutes of returning to the kitchen—jacket on, phone in my hand, as though about to leave—a click and a creak came from the front door, footsteps crossing the living room. I turned to see Mercy standing in the kitchen doorway in joggers and a red sweater, a duffel bag slung her shoulder. "Hello," she said, a smile on her lips.

"Oh, hi." I made my voice casual. "What a nice surprise."

Her face was open and pure. "How funny. I've been thinking of you."

"I—They just left." The shame and excitement of what might happen, what I hoped for, burned under my skin.

She dropped her bag and leaned against the doorframe. "Are you going somewhere?"

"No. I mean, I don't have to."

She smiled again. "Good."

13

THAT'S HOW IT was with Mercy from the beginning. She wanted to be with me. It was that simple.

"Let's get out of here," she said, leaving her bag downstairs next to the freshly made bed. She locked the house and we got in her car.

She said she wanted to pick up something she'd left at her sister's house, which turned out to be barely a mile from mine in the Sunset. Myra was home with her daughters for the second week of their winter break. We found her in the kitchen, stuffing a backpack with sweatshirts and water bottles. "I've been waiting for this week all year," she said. The girls orbited around her, handing her snacks and pulling on socks. I thought of Radhika, bored and restless at Disneyland, impatient to get back to the work that felt, to her, more meaningful and important. This sort of thing was different for different moms. Not good or bad, just different. Myra invited us to join them for a trip to the zoo, but Mercy and I looked at each other and said no, thanks, not this time.

We walked the eight blocks to my apartment under the low winter sun. We made ourselves a late breakfast: toast with jam and butter, another pot of coffee. At the table, Mercy draped an arm over the back of my chair. Not possessive, but confident. Like she already knew what was going to happen.

Later I sat in the armchair while Mercy browsed my bookshelves and asked me questions. Which writers were my favorite? Which ones did I know personally? (Not many.) Which books had I read more than once? More than twice? After a while she took something out of her bag, then came and sat next to me on the carpet, holding it up to show me. It was a copy of my short story collection. "Where did you find that?"

"After we talked that night at Rad's house, I ordered it."

"I'm surprised it's still in print. Please do not feel obligated to read it."

"I already read it." She ran her thumb over the cover. "I loved it. I can't believe it didn't get more attention. Sometimes I really don't understand how the world works."

"Thanks. Me neither."

She asked me about my stories and my childhood. I told her about growing up in Berkeley, how my parents' lives—and therefore mine—orbited the glowing suns of the university, and music, and literature. Their early, incomprehensible deaths, then the quiet years in Toronto with my grandparents. She listened without blinking, every pretense and distraction peeled away, nothing between us but the whites of her eyes and the deep brown of her irises, so dark they merged with her pupils. She was porous, like a sponge. It seemed, after we'd been talking for a while, like I could reach over and squeeze her and everything I'd just said would come dripping out.

"So you're totally alone?" she said. "No siblings? No cousins?"

"Just me."

"Gosh. Well, I'm glad …" She trailed off, chewing on her lip.

"What?"

"I hope this doesn't completely miss the mark. I really can't imagine what it would be like not having any family of your own. I was going to say I'm glad you'll get to start over soon. When the baby comes."

"You didn't miss the mark," I said. "You got it exactly right."

She climbed into the armchair and tucked her body up next to mine. The afternoon was perfectly clear, unobstructed by fog. There were only the seagulls twisting their lazy paths across the sky as the daylight hinged on its shallow axis toward dusk. Mercy twined her fingers loosely in mine, and we kissed—her small, probing tongue, her mouth salty and clean, like a tide pool. After a long time I whispered, "Can you stay here tonight?"

She groaned, pressing her face against my cheek. "I wish I could. But that's kind of the deal with house-sitting: you have to actually sleep there."

"Can I come with you?"

She shook her head. "That's Radhika's only rule when they're away. No guests."

I laughed to cover my disappointment. "What, does she have a nanny cam or something?"

She looked at me very seriously. "Radhika doesn't need a nanny cam. She knows everything."

And so Mercy returned to Radhika's house that night, and I fell asleep imagining her there, in the room with the yellow walls and white sheets. I woke up thinking about her, and then at sunrise she was there, knocking on the door in her sweatpants, holding coffee and a bag of donuts. I took her by the hand and led her to the bedroom, held up the comforter for her to slip in beside me. The coffee went cold on the bedside table.

Afterward we walked on the beach in the low morning sunlight, the wind whipping our hair into our faces and blowing our voices behind us. We had to shout to hear each other. I felt like we were being swept up into something that would carry us together into our shared future.

PART TWO

14

M Y MOM, BEFORE she had me, lost two fingers of her right hand in a climbing accident. This was a very noticeable thing about her. Not the missing fingers, which were easy to overlook, especially in your own mother, but the different way she had of doing ordinary things. Holding a pen (she used a prosthesis that hooked onto the pointer and pinkie), slicing an apple (all our knives had a little top knob to stabilize her grip), typing (an asymmetric click-clack). Fastening a barrette. As a kid I used to dream—and still sometimes do—that a part of my body was missing. An arm, an eye, a leg.

When she became pregnant with me, my mother saw a doctor who raised some concern about her missing fin-gers—whether she would be able to "physically handle" a newborn, whether it would even be safe. She and my father marched out of his office and never returned.

"You clamped onto my nipple and didn't let go for ten months," my mom told me. "You could've dangled there by the strength of your own gums, like a fish on a hook, if you'd needed to." She rolled her eyes. "How many fingers did that man think one needs to hold a baby?"

MERCY AND I saw each other every day that week, the last week of the year. We took long walks, hung around talking, eating, having sex, doing nothing. But it didn't feel like nothing. It felt like something. Everything.

In Myra's living room, Mercy played her cello for me: Bach's third suite. I lay on the floor in a patch of sunlight while Myra's daughters wandered through on their way to the kitchen, ignoring us. They were used to music in their home, the same way I was as a kid. Afterward Mercy wiped the rosin dust off her bow, lay her cello on its side and stretched out beside me on the carpet. "I love that you play music," I said.

She arched her body like a cat, looking at me over her shoulder. "Why did you stop the piano?"

I shrugged. "It wasn't my true love."

"You must've been good."

I made a little face.

"What."

"I don't want you to think of me as childish. Or self-indulgent."

"Come on."

I told her about an argument with my mom after a piano recital. "I'd wanted her to buy me a fancy recital outfit, like the other kids had. There was this one girl who wore these flowy black pants and a little fuzzy sweater with cap sleeves."

"Sounds hot."

I laughed. "It was. I wanted to feel the way that girl looked."

I'd been angry before the recital even started. Somehow the anger made all my self-consciousness fall away, and I found I could play with the kind of passion my teacher was always asking for. "It was the first time I played … not just technically well, but—"

"You rocked it. You were the star."

"I knew I was. And I guess I didn't know how to hide it."

I couldn't see Mercy's face, but I knew she was listening. Her calloused fingertips rested on the back of my arm.

"Afterward I wanted my mom to tell me I'd played better than everyone else. I was being kind of a brat. Finally in the car home I blurted, 'Why can't you just say it? I was the best.' And she just looked at me and said"—I swallowed, the words thick in my throat—"'Josie, you are a very intelligent and creative girl. You will impress many people with your talents. But you're not always very nice.'"

Mercy kept her hand on my arm. After a long moment she said, "But you are so nice."

"No," I said, shaking my head. "It's true. Being nice didn't come naturally. I had to learn it."

"I find that hard to believe." On the carpet, I traced my finger along the edge of sunlight from the window. Its shape moved like someone breathing in their sleep. After a while Mercy said, "So do I get to read your novel now?"

I laughed and rolled away.

ONE EVENING I told Mercy I wanted to cook her dinner.

"Your place?" she said.

"No. Radhika's."

I made the only fancy meal I knew how to cook: mushroom lasagna and kale salad. "Is this always how you seduce younger women?" She leaned against the wide counter.

I poured her a large glass of red wine. "Only the ones I want to impress."

She laughed and took a sip.

The truth was I had cooked the same meal for other women—not many. But I wasn't trying to seduce Mercy, or even impress her. I only wanted to be able to give her something.

Later as I sliced the lasagna, she asked me, "What did your parents know about you?"

"You mean did they know I was queer?"

"That's what I mean."

I gestured with a spatula for her to pass me her plate. "They must have known. I mean, God, I was crawling out of my skin." I thought about this some more. "Sometimes I think my dad's anger might've had something to do with it. They were both, you know, good, progressive people. But they were also of a different generation, and traditional in their own ways." I passed the plate back to her, heavy and steaming.

"Sounds like you've had at least some therapy."

"A long time ago."

She served herself salad. Her hair was down, and her curls kept falling over her eyes. "And what about you and Radhika? Were you ever a couple? In college?"

I laughed at this. "Me and Radhika? No."

"But you were close."

I shook my head and blew on a bite of mushroom. "We weren't, really. I hardly even knew her. She was more like ... someone I watched." I was remembering Radhika in our undergraduate fiction workshops, the way she would sit at the seminar table, one arm slung over the back of her chair, long, dark hair gathered in a ponytail at her neck, eyelashes brushing her cheekbones. She would listen silently through the entire class, making these little movements with her jaw, saying nothing, until finally she would raise one arm in the air. Then the professor would call on her with a look of pleased anticipation, and she would deliver some concise, devastating insight about the manuscript under discussion, cutting to the central problem of the story, the problem we'd all been trying and failing, for the preceding ninety minutes, to articulate. I wanted to describe all this to Mercy, but it felt impossible. I shrugged and said, "The other students hated her. At some point it came out that she wasn't even an English major. She was a molecular biology major and president of the Pre-Med Society. That only made them hate her more."

"But not you."

"No."

"You loved her."

I blew out a breath. The truth was that sex and desire had been sources of interminable confusion for me in college. I thought about sex fairly often, wanted it basically all the time—far more than I did now, in my thirties—whether it was with a man or a woman didn't really matter. "It's going to sound like I'm making this up. I know Radhika is objectively beautiful. But I was never ..." Mercy watched me closely. "I guess you could say I was attracted to her mind."

"And you still are?"

I blinked. "Yes. But not the way I'm attracted to you."

"Psshh." She batted a hand at me.

I poured her more wine. "Enough with the interrogation. Your turn."

She told me about her childhood. She and Myra had grown up in South San Francisco, daughters of a single mom. "We weren't some struggling single-parent household. My mom's a pediatric intensive care nurse. She made good money, and she leaned on her siblings and her parents for help. They all raised us, basically." Then when she and Myra were in middle school, their mom married Steve, a venture capitalist she met in a yoga class. "All of a sudden we were rich and living in Marin County, and everything changed. But in a way nothing changed, too. My mom's solid like that."

Right after high school, Myra went to nursing school and got a job in the ER, where she thrived on the fast pace and adrenaline. She'd inherited their father's intensity and impulsivity. "She married young, had her kids right away. Then she cheated on her husband with some dude she went to high school with."

"Gosh."

"It happened when the girls were really little. Her husband left, and that was it. He's still very involved with the girls, even though he lives in Arizona now. He's a good guy." She wiped the side of her knife against a piece of mushroom on her fork. "She was a wreck for a long time. But it was her own fault, and she knew it."

"You sound like you're the older sister."

"People always used to say that. Because I'm more levelheaded, I guess. But Myra's mellowed out a lot, especially since she became a single mom. Now she's the grown-up."

"And you?" I'd meant to tease her, but her voice was serious.

"It's just that everyone thinks I need to get my life together."

"Who thinks that?"

"My mom, mostly. Even Myra worries about me not having a plan once I move out of Rad's house. She thinks I'm going to be sleeping on her couch like I did after college. Of course I'd be welcome, but you know."

"What?"

"I'm twenty-six."

"So?"

She shrugged. "Only Steve tells them to lay off, let me figure out what I want to do."

"He sounds like a good stepdad."

"Steve's great. He's got my back. But his perspective is kind of privileged. He dropped out of college, messed around for a while, made his millions investing in tech or whatever. My mom has that immigrant mentality, you know: Pick a career. Work hard. Settle down. I respect that."

"But you don't want to settle down?"

She leaned back in her chair. "It's not that I don't want to settle down—or work hard, for that matter. Childcare happens to be the work I love. And it *is* hard. My mom is basically a woke, progressive Mexican lady. She knows I'm queer. She has no problem with that." She shook her head. "But she doesn't want me making a career out of raising other people's kids. To my family, that's not success. They want me to get an advanced degree, become a nurse or a doctor or even a professional cellist. Some version of the 'successful' brown woman who goes to work every day and pays some other brown woman to watch her kids."

"They want you to be like Radhika."

She laughed. "Yes. Exactly. Like Radhika." I heard the bitter edge in her voice. "I'm not saying there's anything wrong with Radhika's life," she went on. "She's really driven to do all her important things: taking care of her patients, writing her book. I tried being driven, too, when I was in that fellowship. And I hated it. I'd honestly rather be chasing after Radhika's or Myra's kids. Someday I want to be chasing after my own kids. I know it sounds like the wrong thing, like you can't be an enlightened feminist in the twenty-first century and say that."

"I think it's admirable," I said. Then I added, "I think Radhika's way is admirable, too."

She raised an eyebrow. "Do you?"

I hadn't expected her to challenge me, and I paused to ask myself if I meant it. I thought of Myra, stuffing backpacks for the zoo. And of my own mother. "I think maybe there isn't a right way to do it. My mom worked a lot when I was a kid. When I was really little, like Saniya and Sachin's ages, I'm pretty sure she slowed down, made some sacrifices. But I was never aware of her choosing between me and her work." Lately I'd been scraping the blackened bottom of my brain for evidence: the balance of her time, her devotion. "I remember tiptoeing down to her office when I couldn't sleep—the same way Rad's kids do with her." Mercy smiled at this. "She was probably just starting to find a balance as I was getting older and, you know, more self-sufficient. But then she fell off a cliff."

Mercy put her hand on mine. "Oh, Josie."

I stared past her, suddenly self-protective. After a moment I took my hand away, picked up my fork and moved some invisible slivers of kale around on my plate. "But back to your life plan. Does Radhika have anything to say about it?"

She eyed me for a moment, then she picked up her fork, too. "You bet she does. She was the one who encouraged me to apply for the fellowship, remember? It's still a source of tension between us. At least I feel it."

"Really? I don't see Radhika as someone who would hold onto something like that."

"You haven't known her that long."

It occurred to me then that July no longer felt so far away. I imagined Mercy leaving Radhika's house, presumably moving back in with Myra, or finding a new family to live with, caring for their children, while I was still alone in my apartment, raising a baby.

Mercy took her napkin from her lap and folded it on the tabletop. "So what kind of advice is Radhika giving you? Has she read your novel? The whole thing?"

I told her she'd read it.

"Not fair." She nudged my foot under the table. I nudged her back. "Have you read the book she's writing?"

"Not all of it, no. She's in a more, um, developmental phase of her process."

"And what phase are you in?"

I found myself telling her more than I'd planned to: Radhika's praise of the not-quite-complete manuscript, her hotshot agent who wanted to read the ending. "But now I have to actually finish it. And Radhika has this very strong principle that she won't touch the ending. She won't even talk about it. She expects me to finish it before the baby comes."

"Ah. That sounds like Radhika. She loves deadlines."

I chewed on the inside of my cheek. "It makes sense though, right? She's a cancer survivor after all."

It was the first time either of us had mentioned Radhika's cancer. For a moment I felt as if I'd told a secret. But of course Mercy knew. She didn't miss a beat. "Sure. And I guess a deadline can be helpful. Even an arbitrary one."

"Well, it isn't completely arbitrary. It's my due date."

"What, so once you're a mom you can't write anymore? Isn't Radhika writing a book?" I sat on my hands for a moment, then tugged them out. Mercy laughed again. "Don't listen to Radhika. Forget the deadline thing, if it stresses you out. Work on it for as long as you want."

"I've been working on it for ten years."

"And are you happy?"

"I was for a while." I set my lips in a straight line. "I'll be happy when it's finished."

"I'll be happy, too." She reached over and hooked her fingers with mine. "Because then I'll get to read it."

I threw her hand back at her, laughing. "Selfish."

THE NEXT AFTERNOON at my apartment, Mercy was squatting in front of the rows of spiral notebooks on the lowest bookshelves. "What are these? Are these the novel?"

"A few of them are," I said. "Early drafts."

"And the rest?"

"They're nothing. Just old diaries."

She stayed crouched there for a moment, as though waiting for me to say more. Then she stood, picked out a slim poetry volume from a higher shelf, read a few pages. I pretended not to watch her.

After a while she put the book back and said she would go get us some lunch. When I heard her footsteps on the stairs in the courtyard, I went over to where she'd been squatting by the bookshelf. I picked up a random notebook and opened it. It was dated six years ago. I hardly recognized the words as mine, even though it was all my own handwriting, my own thoughts. There were notes and ideas for the novel, but also, to my surprise, several random observations and ideas from the things that had been happening at that time. Some descriptions of the weather, inconsequential events and conversations at work, bitter questions and recollections about a long, drawn-out breakup after an even longer, drawn-out relationship. I'd forgotten what it was like to dwell in these lucid, immediate observations, and to believe they were worth writing down, for no other reason than that they'd happened.

I was still hunched over the notebook when Mercy returned. I didn't look up, but I was aware of her sliding a grocery bag off her hip onto the counter, slicing bread, humming quietly to herself. She came into the living room with two plates: turkey sandwiches, sliced pears, dried cherries. We ate sitting cross-legged on the floor, our knees barely touching. After a while she crawled toward me on the carpet and climbed into my lap, kissing me hungrily, slipping her small hands into my underwear. I softened my body into hers.

After she left that night, I sat in the armchair, still with the tart taste of cherries and her lip balm on my mouth. I opened a new, blank notebook, stared at the page for a long time, then picked up a pen, twirling it between my fingers before placing it at the top of the page. I wrote it all down: the tender, languid rhythm of our afternoon together, the melody of her humming voice, the slap of her bare feet on the linoleum, the crunch of toast between our teeth. And against it all, the pleasant awareness of a second, silent heartbeat thrumming inside me.

* * *

THERE'S A DREAM I have sometimes about Mercy—a dream that only started after I lost her, lost all of it.

In the dream she's walking away from me, down an empty beach dense with fog. I can see her ponytail bobbing with each step, and I run to catch up with her. As I get closer I can see that she's bent almost double, clutching something to her chest, bowing her head and hunching her shoulders as though to protect whatever she holds in her arms. *Mercy!* I call out to her, but she doesn't turn around.

Finally I touch her shoulder. *What is that? What are you holding?*

She shakes her head and says only, *Sssshhhh.*

She keeps walking, and I follow her.

Mercy! What is it?

Sssshhhh.

I catch up to her again, and she turns away from me, angling her body toward the ocean.

In the dream I feel a deepening dread, because I'm fairly sure she's holding nothing—and why would she do that? Is she playing some kind of sick game? I keep running after her. Eventually she slows her pace, then stops. She's rocking her arms back and forth, the way a little girl would rock her pretend baby. Playing house. A pulse of anger beats through me.

What is it? What are you holding? I step around her, peering over her shoulder, but again she steps away.

Still not looking up, she gives a harsher, louder, *Sshh!* Then, in a fierce whisper, *You'll wake her.*

Wake who?

She lifts her chin, and as she does, I can see clearly what I already know: her arms are empty. She's holding nothing. Air. She glares at me, and I can see tears in her eyes. *Nivea*, she says, as though it's obvious. As though I'm the one who's crazy.

Nivea. And this is the worst part: In the dream, I have no idea what she's talking about. I just say again, confused, frightened: *Who?*

15

I FORGOT IT would have to end: this strange week outside of time, in which Mercy returned to Radhika's house every night and I lay awake thinking about her, imagining how we would spend the next day, and the next, and the next.

We drove to Mercy's parents' house in Marin County for New Year's Eve. On the Golden Gate Bridge the low afternoon sun outlined the towers, red chalk against blue sky. Tourists hurried in pairs and clusters along the sidewalk, their heads ducked against the wind, some of them peering over the railing at the water below.

My phone buzzed on the center console between us. It was Radhika.

Survived the trip to L.A. On our way home. See you tomorrow?

I put the phone in my pocket and looked out at the sailboats on the water. "Radhika comes home tonight," I said.

"Oh, I'm very aware." She glanced at me. "I put the presents under the tree like you said." I pictured the slim packages the way I'd wrapped them just a week ago: brown packing paper, corners neatly pressed and taped, red string tied in floppy bows. Relics from another era.

The car passed through Robin Williams Tunnel. As we burst back into the sunlight, Mercy shifted her eyes to look at me. "So are we going to keep hanging out once she's back?" Her voice was teasing.

"Why wouldn't we?"

"I don't know. Radhika keeps you pretty busy."

"She keeps you pretty busy, too."

"Nah. I'm my own boss." I touched her leg. She slipped one hand off the wheel and placed it on top of mine. "I don't want this week to end."

"It's not over yet," I said.

She squeezed my fingers. "What are you doing tomorrow?"

I licked my lips. "Actually I'm supposed to go to the matinee concert at the symphony. With Radhika and Adam. I invited them a long time ago." I hesitated, then said, "I wish you could come too. I'm pretty sure it's sold out." I didn't actually know this. I did know I could almost always get an extra ticket to the symphony if I needed one.

"Thanks. I couldn't have come anyway. I've got plans."

I felt secretly relieved. Even after the long, happy week with Mercy, there was still a part of me that wanted Radhika to myself.

"I could hang out after, though," she said, breaking the silence.

"Okay." I knew I sounded noncommittal. "Let's see what time we're both done and text each other."

She glanced at me again. "Okay. Text me." We rode in silence for a while, then she said, "I'm pretty sure I'm in love with you, you know."

I tipped my head back against the seat. "Only pretty sure?"

She laughed. "Mmm. Ninety percent sure. Like maybe I'd need one more full week with you to get to a hundred percent."

My heart lifted up on wings like the birds over San Quentin. "I'm pretty sure I'm in love with you too."

The car curved around the hills on the highway. Then she said, "Are you going to tell Radhika about us?"

"What about us?"

She laughed again.

MERCY'S MOM AND stepdad lived in a big house in Larkspur, with a deep front porch built around a redwood tree. Christmas lights still twinkled in the windows.

Mercy held my hand as she opened the door. Inside, Myra, Mercy's grandmother, and a few aunts were gathered around a kitchen island making tamales while some younger cousins stood nearby, picking at a charcuterie board. Steve and half a dozen uncles were watching a soccer match on TV. From the back porch, one of Myra's kids came running through the open French doors, chasing a Ping-Pong ball as it bounced into the living room.

"Look at you." Mercy's mom floated over to greet us, arms open. "You brought a friend." She kissed me on the cheek and introduced herself as Daniela. She was plump and petite and looked just like Mercy.

Steve stood up from the couch, tall and handsome in a middle-aged way; he couldn't have been more than ten years older than me. I hung back for a moment and watched him with Mercy. They hugged and she whispered something. He laughed, bending forward slightly, nodding, looked her in the eye to ask a question, then turned his ear to her once again. I felt a kinship with him, a feeling that we both recognized something special in this unambitious family woman, this natural, attentive caretaker. When Mercy introduced me, Steve shook my hand warmly. Then he turned to Mercy, his eyes teasing. "So how was your week off? You didn't get bored without any kids to boss around?"

She rolled her eyes. "I bossed Josie around," she said.

"Ah." He wagged a finger. "Josie, look out. She's a no-nonsense babysitter. She takes her job very seriously."

"So I'm learning."

We spent the afternoon and evening that way: chatting with Myra and Mercy's aunts and uncles, playing a few rounds of Ping-Pong and foosball, watching TV with the kids while the tamales steamed. Mercy drank a beer and a couple glasses of wine over dinner. For dessert, Steve brought out a platter of cheeses, sliced apples, and dates. I'd never eaten a date before. Mercy placed one in my mouth and told me to chew out the pit. It tasted like maple syrup.

It's hard to explain, but moments like these are the kind that used to make me miss my parents: trying a new dish, especially one I thought of as upper class and exotic, like cheese and dates for dessert; or flipping through a book on someone else's shelves ("Never heard of it, is it any good?"), only to learn it was considered a classic. I guess it made me wonder whether my parents, had they lived longer, would have exposed me to more experiences and opportunities. Perhaps it's a universal feeling of adulthood: the suspicion that you may have missed out on some core instruction, some foundational knowledge that everyone else seemed already to possess. But sometimes I thought it was unique to orphanhood. I posed this question to Eleanor once, thinking maybe she would know what I was talking about. She just said, "Remember Josie, I left Seoul when I was sixteen. There wasn't much my parents could've helped me with by way of cultural experiences. They barely spoke English. I pronounced the 'c' in *muscles* until I was thirty."

That evening, biting through the flesh of a date, probing out its pit with my tongue, I realized with a sort of surprised relief that I didn't feel homesick for my parents. I had Mercy.

After dessert, Mercy drank another glass of wine and fell asleep on my shoulder while I let Myra's kids show me some videos on her phone. A little past midnight I drove Mercy's car home while she dozed in the passenger seat. We pulled up to Radhika's house in the early hours of the morning. Mercy opened her eyes and touched the side of my face. "Will you come inside?"

"What about Radhika's rule?"

She frowned, her eyelids heavy. "Fuck Radhika."

I wanted nothing more than to curl my body next to Mercy's, feel her knees tuck into the backs of my legs, her forearm slide between my thighs. But I leaned over and kissed her on the cheek. "You're a little bit drunk."

"I am not."

"I'll call you tomorrow after the symphony, okay?"

She dropped her hand to my wrist and let her fingertips rest there. "Yes," she said. "After the symphony."

16

FLOATED INTO Radhika's house just after noon the next day. In a celebratory mood, I'd stopped at an upscale corner market and bought a bottle of sparkling wine. But when I thrust it into Radhika's hands, she looked confused. "I'll fall asleep if I drink this now," she said, and handed the bottle to Adam.

She was in an elegant floor-length dress, midnight blue with a print of giant gold flowers. The shiny fabric clung to her long arms and waist, and the skirt billowed around her as she moved through the kitchen. I was in my usual cardigan and slacks, plus Radhika's shawl, which she'd never told me to keep—I simply hadn't given it back, had instead been wearing it nearly every day while she was gone. When I wasn't wearing it, I kept it folded in my purse like a security blanket.

Adam thanked me for the bottle and placed it in the refrigerator. As the door sucked shut, the kids' footsteps began their rumbling crescendo on the stairs, and then they were in the kitchen, tugging on my arms, telling me about Disneyland.

"Hey guys," Adam prompted, "what do you want to say to Auntie Josie?"

"Thank you for the coloring books!" they chimed.

"Oh, yes, thanks Josie," said Radhika, looking up from her phone. "And for the poetry collection, too. That was sweet of you."

"Have you heard of that poet?" I said.

"No." She wrinkled her nose. "I don't usually read other doctors' writing."

Adam walked behind her and gently squeezed her upper arm. "Inferiority complex."

She shot him a look that I'd only ever seen her give the children. *Watch it.* I could feel the simmering tension in the room, some silent strain between them. I thought of the trip to LA, the long winter break, Radhika's patience wearing thin. Saniya had drifted toward her mother and now hovered at her waist. Radhika absently ran her fingers through her daughter's fine, dark hair. "That's not *why*," she snapped at Adam. "I honestly don't think most doctors write that well."

Then there were footsteps again, and suddenly Mercy was in the room, drying her hands on a towel. How familiar yet surprising she looked to me now, in Radhika's kitchen, wearing joggers and a sweatshirt, hair in a neat ponytail, cheeks flushed. "Hi, nice to see you again," she said to me, a secretive smile on her lips. Her voice was professional and courteous, but her eyes flashed. Of course—what "plans" had I thought she would have while Radhika and Adam and I were at the symphony? This was her home. These were her plans.

"Nice to see you, too." I glanced at Radhika, who was scrolling on her phone again. Saniya left her side and went to Mercy, circling an arm around her thigh. All I could think about was Mercy's tongue in my mouth. I wanted her so badly I could hardly stand up.

Then Adam said we should get going, and Radhika strode toward the garage, pulling on her coat. Saniya whined, "*No*, Mama! I don't want you to go! I want you to *stay*!" Dropping Mercy's leg, she rushed toward Radhika and grabbed for the front of her dress. Radhika thrust out an arm, but Saniya was too quick. She already had a fistful of the shiny fabric in her little hand. With one fierce tug she pulled down on the low neckline, exposing Radhika's lace bra and, for the briefest second, the edge of an ugly brown scar, raised and rough as bark. Radhika yanked the dress up with one hand and, with the other, shoved Saniya away, perhaps harder than she'd meant to. Saniya stumbled back, bumping into Mercy, who steadied her and then held onto her shoulders—like she was protecting her, or protecting Radhika, or both.

I kept my eyes down. For a moment nobody moved. Then Adam said again, "We really should get going." He picked up Radhika's coat from the floor and held it out to her. She slipped into it, shrugging her shoulders back, smoothing the front of her dress. I buttoned my sweater. Mercy lifted Saniya to her hip, murmuring something to her, stern but kind. At the garage door Radhika paused, turned, and strode back into the kitchen. She kissed each of the children silently on the cheek, first Sachin, then Saniya. Saniya threw a hand around the back of her mother's neck and pulled her close, not letting go. Mercy pried her little fingers loose, whispering, "Remember what I said." Saniya's eyes filled with tears, but she didn't cry out. I followed Adam and Radhika into the garage. As I turned to look at back at Mercy, she gave me the tiniest wink, and I felt grateful for her.

I thought I would sit in the back seat of Adam's car like last time, but Radhika said don't be ridiculous, I was pregnant and I was treating them to the symphony, I should ride in front. She climbed into the back and didn't say another word on the short drive. Adam and I chatted innocuously. I asked about their trip to LA and about his parents, whom he described as "aging but stable." He asked about my work at the symphony, and I went on too long, wanting to keep up a stream of conversation to ease the tension that crackled between them. But as we walked from the Civic Center garage to the symphony hall, Radhika's silence fell over all three of us like a spell. A fine mist hung in the air. It seemed like it might rain.

Inside the bright lobby, the sweeping windows overlooked the gray afternoon: Van Ness Avenue with its red center stripe, disappearing over the sharp crest of the cityscape. From our seats in the center of the loge, we peered down on the musicians like birds from a telephone wire.

Onstage, Eleanor looked small and serious with her shining black bangs, pale wrist propping up her violin, eyes trained on the conductor. The first work on the program was Strauss's *Ein Heldenleben,* which momentarily jarred and irritated me with its dramatic blaring of horns and clashing of cymbals. The conductor hopped around and waved his arms like a general directing his troops. But before the intermission, they played Beethoven's Piano Concerto No. 3, and a sense of peace washed over me. I sat perfectly still, hardly breathing, as the second movement swelled and faded to the murmuring piano cadenza. Out of the corner of my eye I could see Radhika's hand resting on Adam's knee. I sensed her shallow breathing, and when I glanced up I saw her face was shining with tears.

AFTER THE CONCERT I used my building pass to slip backstage. I could tell Radhika had been back here before, or anyway she didn't make a show of gazing around and acting awed the way other people did. I introduced her to Eleanor, then mostly listened while the two of them talked about the program (Rad had a firmer grasp of musical history and theory than I expected) and a bit about symphony politics. I could tell whatever had been irritating Radhika had passed, but Adam still seemed distant. While they talked, he wandered off, pretending to look at some old photographs on the walls.

Radhika kept up a stream of chatter in the car. Back at the house, she was relaxed and expansive. "Is anyone else famished?" She rummaged through the freezer and produced a frozen pizza, read the box and pushed some buttons on the oven, all while Adam and I were still hanging up our coats. He wandered off to find Mercy while Radhika peered into the fridge. "I'm ready for that champagne. Where did Adam … Ah!" She lifted the bottle, triumphant. Then, peeling off the foil, she said absently, "That Eleanor Choi is an odd one, isn't she?"

I felt my cheeks get hot. "How do you mean?"

"Well, she's sort of like a child, isn't she? She reminds me of the nerdy Indian kids I grew up with. Bangs in her eyes, super serious."

"I guess she's very dedicated to the work."

"Obviously. But they might want a concertmistress with a little more poise. You get the sense she doesn't leave the house much."

Very calmly, because I could feel the reaction rising inside me, I said, "She's quite cosmopolitan, actually."

She looked up. "Do you know her well?"

"We're friends." Then I added, "Close friends. Practically family."

There was a brief silence. "Well, I only talked with her for a few minutes, obviously." She struggled with the champagne cork. "She seems perfectly nice."

Just then Adam reappeared with Mercy and reported that the twins were already asleep in front of a movie. "Pajamas on, teeth brushed. They just need to be plopped into their beds." He shook his head. "Mercy, I'm going to miss you."

Then there was a bang. The cork shot through the air, hitting the dining room wall. "Bubbles, anyone?" Radhika held up the fizzing bottle and started pouring it into four flutes on the counter. "Mercy, join us?"

Mercy eased onto a stool, her foot brushing against mine. Radhika handed a glass to Adam and gave him a pointed look, like an instruction. He stared at her blankly, or perhaps defiantly, as though resisting what he knew was expected of him. Then, lifting his glass in the air, he said, "To a happy New Year. May it bring us two great books, and"—he seemed to catch himself. He glanced at me, his eyebrows forming a tentative question.

"And one healthy baby," I said, grinning.

"Here here," said Mercy, then gave me another wink over the edge of her glass. Radhika's face was tilted toward the ceiling, but I thought I saw her eyes dart quickly between me and Mercy.

Adam slid the pizza into the oven and started washing lettuce for a salad. Radhika sliced an avocado, her long, tapered fingers working the knife while Mercy and I sat at the counter, not looking at each other. My giddy anxiety began to fade as the few timid sips of champagne fizzled to my head. We ate and talked about music and politics and a debate over kindergarten homework.

"Apparently the teacher at the school where the twins will go next fall gives homework every night," said Radhika, "which Adam thoroughly disapproves of." She threw him a knowing, teasing look.

Adam shook his head. "What is a kindergartener going to learn from some dumb worksheet?"

"It's not about the *content*. It's about giving them something to be accountable for. Teaching them personal responsibility."

Adam smirked. "Radhika's a bootstrap Republican at heart."

She flung an arm at him. "I am not." He laughed and leaned away. "You're *never* too young to learn about personal responsibility," she said.

"You sound like my mom," said Mercy.

"And mine," I said. I didn't really remember my mom harping on personal responsibility. But it was thrilling to align myself, secretly, with Mercy.

"Well, great. That's just lovely." Radhika threw up her hands, but she sounded pleased, almost victorious.

At some point Adam left to scoop the kids off the couch and carry them to bed. He didn't return. No one else seemed tired. Mercy and Radhika refilled their champagne glasses. I let the warmth of the kitchen surround me like a womb. Mercy's cheeks were flushed and she had a smear of pizza sauce on her chin. Radhika kept laughing loudly and holding onto my arm, her feet propped on the edge of my chair, her pretty dress fanning around her ankles. She seemed a little bit drunk. My anger at her earlier meanness faded. It seemed to me in that moment that Radhika and Mercy were both truly generous people—with their time, their friendship, their art. I thought I should learn to be more like them: able to blend my writing into my friendships, my friendships into family. I imagined the same scene a year from now, when I would have my baby in my arms. That evening, for the first time, I began to fully imagine her in this new version of my life. It was like she was already here, and she belonged to all of us.

BY THE TIME the champagne bottle was empty and the pizza devoured, Radhika was starting to yawn. I knew this was my cue to leave. In a moment of desperation I said, "Who's ready to head out to the bars?" It didn't come out sounding as ironically as I'd meant it.

There was a beat of silence. Then Mercy looked straight at me and said, "I'm down."

Radhika laughed at us through another yawn. "Wow. Those days are over for me." Then she shot me a look that seemed somehow mischievous, like a dare. "But go, live it up, Josie. Enjoy your freedom while it lasts."

I glanced back and forth between the two of them. "Okay," I said. "Let's go."

I thought I saw Radhika's face tighten just a little. For a moment I wondered if I should've stayed back with her, clearing the dishes, talking at her kitchen table. But of course she wouldn't want that. It was late, and she was tired. School and the workweek started again tomorrow. It occurred to me that maybe the two-week hiatus in our evening sessions had been the kind of interruption that could break a rhythm, or cure a habit. Maybe the whole "writing partner" thing would fade, and from now on we would just be normal friends who enjoyed each other's company and confided in each other, while the arc of my life bent toward Mercy, and motherhood.

But then Radhika looked me in the eye. "Back to work tomorrow, Josie? I'll see you after your swim?"

And I said, "I'll be here."

Outside, the cold evening felt like the middle of the night, the houses dark and quiet, the streetlamps casting their eerie, buzzing glow. Mercy put her hand in mine. After strolling for a few minutes we came to a block with more lights, restaurants, and bars. Not many people were out. They had done their celebrating already. Ours felt like it was just beginning.

"You sure you're not tired?" Mercy said.

"Nope." I could have stayed up past midnight again. "What about you? Not hungover from last night?"

She laughed at this. "Not at all. I'm still young." I reached over and tugged the curly tip of her ponytail, as though in agreement. She glanced at me, her face shining.

We went into an Irish pub where the air smelled of stout foam and fried food. Quiet music, a gentle female voice—Billie Holiday. Mercy led us to a booth in the back. She slid in after me and we sat with our thighs and elbows touching until our drinks arrived: her beer, my mint tea. We sipped them and said very little. She took my hand, interlacing her fingers with mine under the table. With a little smile on her lips she whispered, "You're going to have a baby."

"I am." We were silent for a while. I wanted to tell her the feeling I'd had on Christmas at Radhika's house—the dread of being the only person my daughter had in the world, the need for a backup plan, another layer of protection—but I didn't know how. "When she's here," I said, "you'll babysit for her, right?"

She turned and looked me in the eye. Then she said, very seriously, "Josie, I don't want to babysit for her."

I held her gaze, which was steely, almost accusatory. I realized that there were tears hovering in her bottom lids, and that she was trying not to cry. After what felt like several minutes, she put her head on my shoulder. I placed the knot of our hands in my lap. We sat that way for a long time. We never let go of each other's hands as we walked out the door and down the block, or as we rode the rattling, hissing bus all the way back to the Outer Sunset. Outside my apartment she kissed me on the mouth, a slow, purposeful kiss. As she pulled away, her lower lip clung to mine. I could smell the sweet yeast of the beer on her breath. I held on to her.

I fell asleep that night wrapped in Mercy's body, her arms around my waist, its subtle, barely perceptible curve. I could already feel the shape of our family forming, its warm outline on the cool, rippled sheets.

17

T HE NEXT MORNING Mercy was up early, leaning over me to say goodbye. I spun toward her, my body twisted in the blanket, and let her kiss my lips.

At work, Eleanor texted me.

Eleanor: thanks for coming for coming yesterday, and for saying hi after.
me: I loved it. I'm so glad we came.
me: What did you think of Radhika?
Eleanor: she was more down-to-earth than I expected. The husband is extremely good-looking. Wow
me: Sure, if you like the tall, rich, handsome type.
Eleanor: ha
Eleanor: r u and radhika having an affair?
me: NO!
me: Definitely not. Radhika is straight as a nail.
me: Why would you think that?

Eleanor: dunno. It's not like you to hang around the rich
and glamorous types.
me: She's helping me with the novel, remember?
Eleanor: o yeah. The novel.

After work I took the bus to the JCC, had a good swim, then
walked to Radhika's house, a wool cap over my damp hair.
For the first time in weeks, I wasn't shivering.

At the kitchen table, as I pulled out the latest marked-up
chapter of the manuscript, Radhika said, "So what was all
that last night with you and Mercy?"

"All of what?"

She waited a beat. "She knew you were pregnant."

I straightened my pile of printed pages and said softly,
"So did Adam."

This seemed to catch her off guard. Her voice was defensive, almost annoyed. "I'm sorry, Josie. It came up. I couldn't
lie to him. Besides, you've started showing." My hand flew
to my navel. "Anyway don't change the subject."

I rolled my eyes, secretly pleased to return to the topic
of Mercy. "We hung out a few times while you were gone."

"Josie." Now she dropped her jaw, leaning forward. "Are
you *dating* my *babysitter*?"

I looked at her and tried to keep a serious face, but her
eyes were sparkling and mischievous, and I smiled in spite
of myself.

"Do you want to tell me about it?" she said, laughing.

"I guess we just really enjoy each other's company." I
blushed. "I didn't stay here. She said no guests."

"You're not a guest."

I paused to show that I'd registered and appreciated
this. Then I said, "I know she's young. But I do think she's

incredibly mature." Radhika nodded. Feeling encouraged, I went on. "And she's really got a gift with kids. As you know."

Radhika seemed to reappraise the situation, then. She looked like she was choosing her words carefully. "Look, Josie. I'm not questioning that you and Mercy have a genuine attraction and connection to each other. That's very clear. It was obvious to everyone last night, from the second she walked in the room."

"It was?"

She gave a half smile, lips touching. "You're both wonderful people, so I can see why …" She trailed off. "But like you said, Mercy is very young." The way she said it made it sound like a euphemism for something. "This is a time in your life to be *deliberate* about your decisions. For your own sake, but even more for the sake of your baby."

I smoothed the stack of papers in front of me. "You're trying to protect me from getting hurt."

"Yes," she said. "Because I care about you."

I looked at the table. I wanted to tell her that I cared about her, too. But I couldn't think of a way to say this that didn't sound like I was trying to reassure her that she was still my favorite.

"Josie," she said, and I looked up. She sighed. "What is going on with the novel? It's been two weeks. Did you write an ending?"

For several seconds I said nothing. In the kitchen, the dishwasher pulsed and hummed. "Not yet."

"I guess you've had other things on your mind."

I wanted to slap her. Instead I said, "I still think it would be helpful to brainstorm together. Talk through some possibilities."

She shook her head. "No. We discussed this. That's your work, not mine."

"I'm not asking you to write it for me." I hated the sound of my own voice. "I'm just asking for your help."

"I'm *trying* to help you, Josie. But you have to accept the help I'm offering." She held my gaze, her jaw tight. "You've got six months. That's still a long time. If you stay focused."

"Six months is not a long time." I pouted. "Six months is nothing."

She looked down, then, and in the shadow of her brow I could see that I'd hurt her. Once again my mind flashed to what I so easily forgot: Time, in Radhika's life, had its own meaning. Every single day was something that had been taken away, then given back to her. Six months wasn't nothing. It was everything.

I let out a breath. "I'm sorry, Rad. I know you're trying to help. And I want your help. I just want so badly to get it right."

She looked at me, her eyes big and calm. "You are getting it right. I promise you are."

And there it was—the thing I wanted so badly from her: her confidence, her absolute conviction that I was capable, special, worthy of what she had to offer.

I gave a timid smile that I hoped would restore our usual peaceful symbiosis. "I guess I just need you to remind me of that every once in a while."

She lifted her eyes to mine. "Okay," she said. "I can do that." But I thought I sensed a weary relief in her voice, like someone who's managed to escape a pointless argument with an unreasonable child.

"I'll stay focused," I said. "I promise."

I STARTED TO tell other people about the pregnancy. My symphony colleagues offered their surprised congratulations. The ladies at the pool fawned over me, turning me sideways in my swimsuit. Radhika was right: I was starting to show. A few of them brought me gifts wrapped in pink tissue paper, pressing them on me in the locker room or at the edge of the pool: crib sheet sets, play mats, little pink-and-white outfits from Baby Gap. They wanted to know who the father was. "There is no father," I tried to explain. "There's a sperm donor."

"So you'll be all on your own?" they asked, concerned.

"Not exactly," I said. "I've got a great girlfriend."

Once Eleanor knew about Mercy and the baby, she was effusively excited for us. She wanted to meet Mercy. She wanted to knit me a pair of baby bootees. "Do you knit?" I said.

"No, but I've always wanted to learn."

On the last Friday in January, Eleanor invited me and Mercy to one of Mark's string quartet concerts. The three of us shared a car from Davies to the Unitarian Universalist church in Japan Town. It was a simple building, white walls and wooden beams, a wide vaulted ceiling, a twisted bare branch hung over the altar in place of a cross. Mark was as handsome and humble as ever, black hair combed back, cello balanced against his breastbone. In the simple church, the music was especially stirring. Mercy kept her fingers laced with mine.

Afterward we went out for drinks and sushi. Eleanor and I ordered diet Cokes. I took a few sips from Mercy's beer.

"She's great, Josie," Eleanor whispered to me when Mercy was in the bathroom. "I'm happy for you." Little sushi boats rotated past us at eye level. She grabbed a dish of edamame and popped off the plastic lid, gesturing for me to eat something.

"Do you think it's crazy of me to want to raise this baby with her?" I said.

"You guys are in love. You can't predict the future, right?" She slid an edamame pod through her teeth. "Sometimes you've just got to keep your eyes open and see where things take you."

ON AN UNUSUALLY warm Sunday in February, when the dandelions bloomed and plum petals drifted from the trees, Radhika invited me for an impromptu picnic.

> We'll be at Crissy field in 20 minutes. Picking up an extra sandwich in case you can join.

I slapped my notebook shut and got in a cab. It was Mercy's day off, and I knew she was at Myra's house. We had plans to see each other that evening. I thought about asking her to come along, but I decided against it. I wanted Radhika to myself.

Radhika brought a picnic of banh mi sandwiches, chocolate chip cookies, and lemonade. She seemed energized and unusually relaxed. The kids were happy too, gorging on goldfish crackers and cookies. Only Adam was subdued. He'd seemed that way since the symphony, his brow permanently furrowed below his high forehead. Lying back on the blanket with his long arms crossed behind his head, he barely looked up when I arrived. While we ate our sandwiches, he sat gazing into the distance, chewing thoughtfully.

After lunch Radhika told the kids she was going to teach them to throw a Frisbee, and they spread out across the grass while Adam and I stayed behind on the blanket to watch. She ran tirelessly back and forth, demonstrating proper throwing technique, the elegant curve of her arm mimicking the arc of the Frisbee as it caught the air. Her throws were perfect. Most of Sachin and Saniya's throws sent the Frisbee careening at sharp angles into the trees, or straight into the grass.

Without Radhika's voice to fill the empty space between us, Adam seemed unnaturally quiet. I remembered Thanksgiving dinner, when he'd engaged me so warmly and effortlessly. Maybe this was another kind of intimacy: the silence of two people so comfortable together they didn't have to talk. The silence of family.

With the sun on my neck and bare arms, I felt happy and, I suppose, bold. I shot Adam a long, fearless look, and I heard myself asking the question I never would have asked Radhika. "She's through with it, isn't she?" A gust of wind blew into my face, whipping my words into the air as soon as they left my mouth. But he heard me.

He'd been squinting into the sun, watching his wife and children. Now he half turned toward me, his face good-humored but guarded, his eyes still on her. "Through with what?"

I said, "I mean—just look at her. She looks like the picture of health."

Radhika bounded past us, Frisbee in hand, shouting some instruction to the kids. Adam turned his whole body, now. His eyes roamed over me. If he'd been a different man, in a different place, I would have felt embarrassed under his gaze. I suppose he was sizing me up, in a way. Maybe he was wondering how smart or cunning I was, how deeply I'd already burrowed into the dim, underground tunnels of his wife's consciousness.

"What has she told you?"

I was aware of wanting to manipulate him, to make him think I knew more than I did. But I was also wary of trying to pass anything over on Radhika. I recalled what Mercy had said. *She doesn't need a nanny cam.*

"I know about her cancer."

He looked unimpressed, even amused. "You and every other *Atlantic* subscriber."

Stung, I said, "And we talk about her book, of course." Although this wasn't really true.

"Anything else?" Although his voice was friendly, I could sense that my mission was futile. He belonged to Radhika. When it came to certain private matters, they shared a secret, impregnable allegiance that excluded me, even while they tolerated my company. Suddenly I felt foolish and alone.

From the grass, there was a shout from Saniya. Her voice had a new, biting edge. We both turned to look. Radhika was holding the Frisbee high above her head while Saniya jumped wildly for it, stretching her skinny arms and legs. It was clear from Radhika's face that this wasn't a game. Something had angered her, probably some misbehavior from Saniya. She was done playing. A few feet away, Sachin was tightening the Velcro straps on his shoe, oblivious to their struggle.

Adam seemed to decide to let their conflict run its course. He rubbed his eyes with the heels of his hands. "I don't know if you've figured this out yet," he said, "but there's no point trying to understand Radhika. You'd think she'd be an open book, so to speak." He shook his head. "She's got these clear principles, these things she's so sure about."

I heard the flash of bitterness in his voice, and I flinched slightly. Whatever it was he was telling me, I wasn't sure I wanted to hear it.

"But she's not as rational as she makes herself seem." Then he gave a quiet, rueful laugh. "Maybe none of us are."

"*Mama!*" Saniya jumped in the air, her back arching with useless effort. Radhika's voice had gone low and quiet; we could only see her shaking her head, firm and resolved as ever. "*Mama!*" Saniya was shrieking now.

"She's a black box," Adam said, his voice low and dark. "Even to me."

It occurs to me only now, all these months later, that Adam must have believed I was in love with Radhika. How could he not have believed it? A single, queer, pregnant woman huddled with his beautiful wife every night while he worked and the children slept? It would've been a totally reasonable assumption. Maybe he was more strategic than I gave him credit for. The things he said, the things he didn't.

Stretched out on the picnic blanket that afternoon, I waited for him to keep talking. But he was finished. The two of us just sat there, listening to Saniya's shrieks and cries over the rushing wind, and watching Radhika, silhouetted against the too-bright sunlight, tall and strong as a mountain, her hand raised in the air, holding what her daughter wanted just beyond her reach.

18

THE JANUARY AND February holidays, once unbearably dull and lonesome, now felt luxuriant and joyful. Mercy spent more and more time in my home and in my bed. Weekends were oases of togetherness, our bodies, our plans. Meanwhile, at Radhika's house, life revolved around the monthly calendar hanging over the kitchen table, its icons and rituals. Alongside the arbitrary benchmarks of the pregnancy—the prenatal appointments, the lopsided trimesters—my memories of that time are anchored by whatever holiday was approaching or receding, the kids' construction paper projects on the walls.

The night before Valentine's Day, Radhika brought me along on a last-minute errand. She'd forgotten to buy cards for the kids' preschool classmates. "I'm sorry, this is such a waste of time," she said as we climbed in the car. "You really don't have to come."

"Are you kidding? I can always use a trip to Target. Especially in the car. Maybe I'll buy a full-length mirror."

She laughed. "Or a flat-screen TV."

"Or a Hula-Hoop."

We pulled into the underground garage just as an old, rusted sedan wheezed into a nearby parking spot. As we walked past it a moment later, I saw Radhika's jaw tighten. She nudged me and pointed to a sticker on the rear bumper: CHOOSE LIFE. The two "O"s were a pair of baby footprints curved toward each other.

"My absolute favorite," she muttered. "Moralizing to women on a bumper sticker."

I realized I had placed a hand instinctively on my lower abdomen. I made a little murmuring sound of agreement.

Just then the sedan's driver-side door opened. Radhika slowed almost to a stop, swiveling her neck to look. A middle-aged man with disheveled hair and a scruff of beard emerged from the driver's seat, uncurling his back in the way of the very old or arthritic. He wore a crew-neck sweatshirt with frayed collar and cuffs, ill-fitting jeans, gray tennis shoes. He must have felt Radhika glaring at him, because he looked up. I wonder if he met Radhika's eyes. I shudder to think what he would have seen there. She whispered loudly in my ear, "Doesn't that look like someone whose advice you want on your sexual and reproductive decisions?"

I gave a quiet laugh, but I also felt a pang of something, some pain or sadness I'd caught in the man's tired eyes. I turned back to look, hoping he hadn't heard her. He'd circled to the other side of the car and now hovered at the passenger door, where another, younger man was climbing out.

Radhika strode ahead of me toward the escalators, but I lingered, watching the two men as they shuffled through the dark garage. When they passed an overhead light, I could see unmistakably what they were: a father and his grown son. The same sloping shoulders, the same boxy head and small paunch over their belts. The son wore a hoodie and jeans, ratty tennis shoes like his dad's. I couldn't place his age. He could've been twenty-five or forty-five. He had the unmistakable thick, humped neck and bunched facial features of the congenitally disabled. His eyes squinted through thick glasses, his forehead seemed to push his eyes and nose and mouth together near his chin. His jaw was slack, his smiling mouth hung open. His father kept a hand lightly on his back as they walked; then, stopping by a row of shopping carts, he murmured something. The son nodded and began maneuvering the nearest cart out of a long, nested line. The cart was a bit stuck; he jiggled it—frustrated, ineffective. The father watched him struggle for a moment, then, with a tenderness almost too sweet to bear, touched his elbow and stepped behind him, their arms making parallel lines as they both gripped the handlebar and, with a little jerk, wrestled the cart free. In a brief, almost imperceptible moment, I saw the son tilt his head, touching his ear to his father's shoulder.

I turned away. Radhika was already marching up the escalator with her long legs. I hurried to catch up.

Back in the garage ten minutes later, Valentine's cards in hand, we passed the car with its bumper sticker. I saw Radhika glance at it again and roll her eyes.

I decided to tell her what I'd seen, doing my best to describe the son. "He was, you know, obviously handicapped. I mean mentally and physically." She listened impatiently, as though she already had an answer for whatever I was trying to explain.

"Mm-hmm," she said, when I'd finished. "And I'm sure his dad loves him and can't imagine his life without him. He should get a bumper sticker that says: '*We* chose to have a child with a chromosomal anomaly.' Or, '*We* love our son.' But his experience doesn't give him the prerogative to tell *me* what to do with *my* body and *my* family."

Of course she was right. I wished I hadn't brought it up. There was something about the whole thing, anyway, that I hadn't been able to convey: the father's gentle touch, and the love that pulsed between them like an electric field.

We got in the car and drove away, the children's valentines in my lap. BE MINE. YOU'RE COOL. WE'RE SPECIAL FRIENDS.

THE FOLLOWING WEEK Mercy came with me to my second-trimester ultrasound. Through a pool of cold gel, the technician's magic wand revealed her to us: my baby, in all her fuzzy, alien divinity. We counted her fingers and toes. The tech measured the diameter of her skull, the length of a single toothpick-size femur, the red and blue pools of blood in her four-chambered heart. "Perfect, perfect," she kept murmuring, as she scrolled and clicked with her confident, dexterous fingers. From the side of the table, Mercy squeezed my hand.

It was like walking by a bright window on a dark night and seeing a family gathered around a dinner table, the most intimate scene on unexpected display. Lying on my back, I tried not to stare, awestruck, through the portal this magic wand had opened for me. But I couldn't resist. *This is our family*, I reminded myself. *This is my daughter, my body. I don't need permission to be let inside. She is in me.* My whole being tingled with curiosity and joy and disbelief, and I began to feel light, almost translucent, as though I were being led up a stairway into the clouds, through the gates of some glorious and unimagined heaven.

19

THE ONE DEFECT in my happiness, like a thread tugging a piece of silk, was the unspoken, triangular tension between Radhika, Mercy, and me.

Mercy was never jealous. She never resented my evening sessions with Radhika, which began just as her workday was ending. "This is your work," she said. "I'll be waiting for you when you're done." She still sometimes slept at Radhika's house. But most nights, after catching a glimpse of her leading Sachin and Saniya upstairs in their pajamas, or hearing the soft murmur of their bedtime stories, I would come home to find Mercy in my bed. She would put her book down or close her laptop and open her body to me. Then she would get up before dawn and be back at Radhika's house in time to fix the twins' breakfast. We were entwined in this way, the threads of our lives and schedules tangled in a knot that felt messy and real, like family.

And yet I felt myself holding back from her, particularly those things I shared with Radhika. The novel. The picnic at Crissy Field. The dad and his son in the Target parking garage—I almost told her about that one many times. She would've understood; it would've been a relief to tell her. But I held on to it as though it were Radhika's and my special secret, even though it was a secret whose significance Radhika never really grasped, had probably already forgotten about.

In fact, I had another secret, one that I was keeping from Radhika: I wasn't writing. Of course I wasn't. I didn't need to, didn't really want to. Strange, because writing had never felt like a burden. It had been a necessity, a buffer against the void of my own solitude. And now I was squeezing it in for Radhika's sake, out of some sense of obligation to finish what we'd started.

Sometimes I would bring my laptop to work, skipping my swim in order to hammer out revisions before heading to her house. A few times, knowing there was no way to produce any satisfactory work in the time I had left, I texted her with some vague, last-minute excuse.

Nauseated again. I think I'd better go straight home.
Bad headache. I must not have drunk enough water today.
Sorry, Rad. I'm just not feeling up to it.

I hardly ever mentioned Mercy's name. But there wasn't a second when I wasn't thinking about her, longing to get back to her, even as I jealously protected my time with Radhika. I certainly never mentioned to Radhika that Mercy and I were talking about living together, raising the baby together. I told myself it shouldn't matter to her, anyway, as long as I got my work done and didn't waste her time.

"What do you mean? Of course it matters to her," Eleanor said one afternoon. It was the first weekend of March, a rare Saturday when she didn't have a concert or a dress rehearsal. We met at the steps down to Ocean Beach. She was wearing a wide-brimmed visor and a green surgical mask. I didn't say anything about the mask. It was usually best to tread lightly with Eleanor about these things.

"But why?" I said. "Because Mercy's her nanny? Because Mercy's so young? Because we're gay? What specifically would bother her about it?"

"I have a feeling," Eleanor said, pumping her arms, looking straight ahead, "that for all her emphasis on individual autonomy, Radhika actually has fairly strong opinions about other people's life choices. I don't think yours are any exception."

"I'm pretty sure Radhika has more pressing things to think about."

"I disagree. In fact I think she might feel quite invested in you."

"I can't imagine why."

Eleanor glanced at me from under the brim of her visor. "She spends a lot of time working with you on your novel. Just like she spent a lot of time grooming Mercy for that fellowship."

"You think she's grooming me? Like some kind of predator?"

"I think she sees something in you that she relates to and cares deeply about."

I was secretly pleased Eleanor had this impression—that Radhika cared deeply about me, and my life. It was what I wanted, even though it was becoming inconvenient, even a little oppressive.

We walked on, stepping over tangles of seaweed and driftwood. Wiry joggers passed us in both directions. I changed the subject. "So are you, um, worried about that virus?"

Eleanor kept her eyes off mine, the way she did when her fears and compulsions were at their worst. "It's not just in China anymore, Josie. They say it's only a matter of time until it gets here. Maybe it's already here."

"Maybe. But probably not right this minute on Ocean Beach. Right?"

"I'm just more comfortable with the mask."

"Okay," I said. We kept walking.

A WEEK LATER I was back at Radhika's house. The kitchen walls were covered in shamrocks and leprechauns. We were looking over some of my rushed, half-hearted revisions and eating leftover Indian food at her kitchen table. I polished off every take-out container. Well into my second trimester now, I was always hungry.

As we were finishing up Radhika said, somewhat out of the blue, "We booked our tickets for Chicago for the summer." I waited. I had the feeling she had something to tell me that I wasn't ready to hear. "Has Mercy talked with you about her plans for July? For after we leave?"

"Not lately," I said.

"Me neither. I'm a little concerned that she's ... procrastinating."

"I don't know if she's made specific plans," I said carefully.

"What do you think are the chances she'll get back to playing music seriously?"

I twirled a pen around my finger. It seemed duplicitous to be talking with Radhika about Mercy's professional ambitions, or lack of ambitions. I found myself wanting to portray Mercy in a favorable light, or what Radhika would consider favorable. "Sometimes she talks about starting her own music studio. Teaching lessons."

"Teaching lessons to whom?"

"To kids, I think."

Radhika arched her elegant eyebrows. "Really? As her full-time job?"

"No," I said, feeling bolder now. "Evenings and weekends, just for a little extra income. When she's not taking care of the baby."

Her eyebrows fell and she tipped her chin down. "Are you and Mercy talking about getting married?"

"Not marriage, necessarily." I forced myself to keep my eyes on hers.

She blinked, but she didn't look away. "Josie, can we talk about this?"

Here it was: the snag in the fabric, the thread that had to be pulled loose. I braced myself, preparing to face her. "Sure. Let's talk about it."

She took a breath, and her face twisted a bit. "I'm honestly a little worried about you."

Instead of feeling annoyed at this, I felt strangely moved. "Worried about me?"

"I know you and Mercy are in love. That's very clear. But Mercy is young. Playing house probably seems like fun, now, but—"

I felt a spark of anger. "Come on, Rad. Seriously? We're not 'playing house.'" I'd imitated her slashing air quotes, and now I dropped my hands to my sides. "Do you even hear how patronizing and homophobic that sounds? We're two adults who want to share our lives and raise a child together."

She blinked. "I'm sorry, Josie. You're right." She rubbed the side of her cheek like she'd been punched. But she kept her eyes on mine. "I think because of everything Adam and I went through in my first pregnancy—the cancer, the abortion—I might be transferring some of my fear from those days onto you. Fear that he would leave me, that he would decide it wasn't worth it."

I was so taken aback by this vulnerability and insight on her part, I said nothing for a long time. I just stared at her. It was one of the few but critical times when Radhika showed me that she was capable of being both deeply honest and ruthlessly self-aware. It is still how I think of her.

I decided to try again. "Fine. Apology accepted." She smiled, looking almost chastened. "But given that I don't have cancer, and that Mercy and I are in no way the same as you and Adam, what exactly are you worried about?"

She seemed to regain her confidence. "You know exactly what I'm worried about. You haven't been working on the novel."

Now it was my turn to feel chagrined. "I'm working on it. We're working on it right now."

"You know what I mean. You haven't been putting in the time on your own. Not the way you used to. And I don't think it's just because of Mercy. I can sense a change in you. You've lost your focus. You don't want it as much as you did before."

I swallowed. She was right, and I hated her for it. *I do want it,* I heard myself protest. But even in my head it sounded unconvincing. It was the voice, I realized with a jolt, of my nameless main character, who wanted so much to be someone's daughter, yet could not bring herself to take the necessary risks, to be bold—elbowing others aside, insisting on her own primacy—the way everyone around her was willing to do. Because there was something she wanted more: to be the good, blameless girl her parents would have loved and admired.

A whole new wave of sadness washed over me then, for the book, and for the idea that this girl, this character, might never be known by the world. I suppose it was also a sadness for myself—that I might never be known in the way I wished to be, as a writer. Maybe I, too, was afraid of risk and confrontation. Maybe that was why someone like Radhika was always going to succeed, seemingly without trying. She didn't insist on being blameless. She wasn't afraid to show her choices and their consequences to the world. Whereas I was so busy trying to please everyone else—some invisible audience that was both embodied by Radhika and, I knew, had a life and a power of its own—that I could never create anything truly original and good.

Suddenly I felt very tired. This was precisely what made a friendship with Radhika so rewarding and so taxing. She critiqued everything, distilled every little thing to its truest, undeniable source. There was no hiding from her discernment and her high standards.

"I'm happy," I said weakly. And even though it was true, I could hear how unconvincing this, too, must've sounded to her. A question instead of a statement.

"Were you unhappy before?"

"No. Not at all. I'm the happiest I've been in a long time—and I don't just mean because of Mercy. I mean working on the novel, working with you. These past five months,

I've had this feeling of purpose and, I don't know, confidence, I guess. But now I'm finding that there are other things I want to work on besides the novel, other things that are more important to me, at least right now. Like the baby. And Mercy."

"Josie," she said, a fine tremor in her voice, "Do you understand how drastically your life is going to change once this baby comes? Do you realize how much harder it will be to do *anything*, to achieve *anything*, no matter how much you want it, no matter how hard you work? I know you're in love with Mercy, and that probably seems like the most important and exciting thing in the world right now. But I don't want you to lose sight of this *opportunity*. It's a window of opportunity, and it's closing. You're never going to get it back."

She could be so persuasive. I could almost see it: The window of opportunity. It was the size and shape of the west-facing window in my apartment. I imagined it collapsing on itself, narrowing to a bright, blinding slit, then disappearing.

But then I remembered what Mercy had said, and I shook myself. "I know it'll be hard. But it's not impossible. You're doing it, right? Plenty of people do it. I'm not talking about 'having it all.' I know it's about compromise and …"

When I faltered, she broke in like a bulldozer. "Compromise and sacrifice, blah blah blah. You'll give up some things, but you'll gain something else. Is that what you're going to tell me?" Her nostrils flared and she ground her teeth audibly, bone on bone.

Again it came back to me: everything she'd been through, how different it all must look through the lens of her singular, harrowing experience. I couldn't win this argument with her. Maybe I didn't want to. Shakily, I said, "I've still got four months. I've still got time."

"Yes," she said. "You've got time. But you have to use it well."

THAT NIGHT I got off the bus a few stops early and walked past my neighborhood bookstore, stopping at the window, letting my eyes roam over the display shelves. I imagined my book there, and I felt that rush that had carried me through all those evenings at Radhika's kitchen table, a sort of fearful and wonderful thrill. It was impossible sometimes to distinguish between what I really wanted, and what I wanted because someone else wanted or expected it for me.

Recently Mercy had remarked on my "passivity" around Radhika. "I see the way you are with her. You let her kind of, like, tell you what to write."

"That's not true," I said. "She's very intentional about not telling me what to write."

"Okay, then, telling you what to think."

We were lying on our backs in my bed, our fingers twined together. "I value her opinion immensely," I said. "I trust her."

"Why do you trust her?"

I thought about this. After a while she wiggled her wrist, shaking my hand gently with hers. "Tell me about the abortion in college."

"What do you want to know?"

"I don't know, Josie. Tell me the story."

I rolled onto my side to face her. "I was an idiot. It was senior year. I was drunk at a party. Some guy from one of my English seminars was there. I guess I thought I was seducing him."

"Oh dear."

I winced. "It was literally the first and only time a man put his penis inside me."

"Ugh." She buried her face in my arm. "Penises. Who needs them."

I told her the obvious things: the missed period, the free test from the student health clinic. When I saw the two blue lines, the first thing I did was vomit into a trash bin. Then I vomited again, and again. I had whiplash by the time I picked up the phone.

I don't know why I didn't just call Planned Parenthood like any other pregnant college girl. That's what they were there for; that's why the clinic was a twelve-minute drive from campus. But I knew Radhika volunteered as a patient escort. I suppose even in the midst of my crisis, I saw an opportunity. I called her.

"It was totally out of character for me. 'Reaching out,' as you young folks call it, isn't something I normally do, even when bad things happen. Especially when bad things happen."

"Miss Independent," Mercy whispered.

"Lessons from the school of orphanhood," I said.

And this was where it got strange. On the phone, I told Radhika I hadn't yet decided what I was going to do. Even though I absolutely knew. It hadn't crossed my mind to keep it, not for one second. "But I played the role of this distraught, uncertain girl. I let her counsel me, console me, tell me that only I could make this decision, and that she trusted me without reservation to make it. 'Lots of women do this,' she said. 'It doesn't make you a terrible person.' I had never thought it would make me a terrible person."

She booked the appointment for me: eleven o'clock on a Saturday morning, right after my work-study shift at the pool.

In the lifeguard tower that morning, watching the few early swimmers slice through the water, I thought, *I'm pregnant right now. But in a few hours, I won't be pregnant anymore.*

In the clinic waiting room I read *A Portrait of the Artist as a Young Man.* Radhika flipped through biochemistry flash cards and an MCAT study guide. Eventually someone called my name.

"Do you want to know the gestational age?" the nurse asked as she swept the probe sideways through my vagina.

"Yes."

She clicked a button, then another. "Eight weeks. We can do the procedure today."

Someone placed an IV in my arm. Someone else asked me to undress and cover my lap with a paper drape. Then the doctor walked in, a soft-spoken, middle-aged woman in blue scrubs. She injected some medicines into my IV and the rush of it washed over me. I let my eyes close, only opening them at the strongest, most surprising sensations: the cold blade of the speculum, the sting of the air. The deep, piercing cramps. Then the bizarre feeling of my insides being tugged and yanked for a few intensely uncomfortable minutes, while the doctor said, "Almost done now. Very normal cramping, here. That's all normal. Okay, now it's over. You'll feel a little bit of blood and soap trickle down as I remove the speculum."

Then I was empty, all the cold, prying instruments released from inside me. I opened my eyes, watched the ceiling move in lazy circles, closed them again. I pressed my knees together. A slow, warm thread of blood traced the curve of my bottom. A nurse helped me clean myself and get dressed. She held my underwear as I stepped in, one leg at a time.

I sat on a bench in the parking lot while Radhika went to get her car. The hot, breezy morning had turned cool, a thin layer of cloud obscuring the heady sun. Dried wisteria blossoms from an overhead vine swirled around my feet while a man on the corner, who must not have recognized me as the same person he'd yelled at three hours earlier, implored me to "Turn around! Flee these murderers who would send you and your baby to a hot and eternal hell!"

After that, in the few remaining weeks before graduation, Radhika sat next to me in our advanced fiction seminar every day, even when other seats were open. She looked me in the eye, engaged me in conversation, occasionally whispered in my ear or nodded in agreement with something I said. Sometimes I circled a hand around her arm, leaned over, whispered something back—it didn't matter what. I could feel our classmates watching us. I knew they envied me. I would've been envious, too, if I were them.

In bed that night, after returning from Radhika's house, I pulled out my phone and read the email from Sarah Marshall for the thousandth time. *Mesmerizing. Sharp and original.* I shifted from one side to another, drumming my fingers across my belly, trying to ease a dull ache in my lower back and a wave of nausea quivering in my throat—the palak paneer, maybe, or the adrenaline rush of pushing back against Radhika.

Without meaning to I slipped into my old nighttime habit of reimagining the novel from beginning to end, rearranging the plot around yet another arc of meaning. I felt an urge I hadn't felt in a long time, to flip on the light, grab a notebook, and begin scribbling sentences on the page.

But this was quickly replaced by a different, stronger urge: the palak paneer, plus the spicy pakora and tamarind chutney, churning in my stomach, then clenching into a painful cramp. I rushed to the bathroom. It wasn't vomit that came out of me but diarrhea, a horrible rush of it. For a moment, staggering back to bed, I felt relieved. But as soon as I lay down the pain reared up again, searing and vicious. I don't know how much time had passed when I realized I was holding my arms across my stomach, moaning. I got up to try pacing, but I barely made it to the doorway before sinking to my hands and knees. From there I crawled to the living room carpet. In the dim glow of the streetlamp through the window, I attempted the comforting, alternating rhythm of cat-cow pose, arching and curling my back until I had to sink flat again, draping my belly across my knees. By the time the sky was beginning to lighten I was motionless on my side, groaning each time the pain clutched me again. From far away there was a knocking, and then the creak of the front door. It was Mercy, wearing sweats and carrying a pink pastry box.

She took one look at me and drove me to the hospital.

20

I N THE CAR Mercy stole short, tight glances at me in the rearview mirror. Curled in the back seat, I could see the sliver of a moon hanging in the dim predawn sky, like a piece of white string. I closed my eyes. Opened them again. Watched the tops of buildings and power lines pass at upside-down angles. Finally the big, red signs for the hospital flashed past. The car slowed to a stop. In the stillness, the ticking of the turn signal. We rounded a corner, stopped again. The engine went off. Neither Mercy nor I said anything. She looked over her shoulder, touched my arm. "We're here." I nodded, closed my eyes again, gritted my teeth against another surge of pain.

At the big glass doors to the emergency room, a badged, broad-shouldered nurse stood with her hands on hips, blocking our path. She said, "I'm sorry, but there are no visitors allowed."

I looked at Mercy and saw a shadow of anger cross her face. She lifted her chin, ready to dismiss this nurse and her prejudices. "I'm her partner," she said. "She's pregnant with our baby. I'm coming in with her."

"I understand, and I'm sorry." The nurse's voice was gentler, now, and kind. In a moment of clarity I saw that she had a rainbow flag pinned to her badge. "The rule applies even to partners of pregnant women. There are new infection control measures, new visitor policies. Because of the virus."

I barely knew what she was talking about. I felt dizzy, standing there, listening to the two of them go back and forth.

"She's not sick," Mercy said. "She's pregnant and in pain. Something is wrong."

The nurse's mouth became a line, stern and sad. "I'm sorry," she said again. "She'll have to go alone."

A hospital aide appeared in a pastel-blue vest and a mask, pushing a wheelchair. The nurse helped me into it and draped a blanket across my lap. I writhed in the stiff square of the seat, and I said to Mercy from what felt like a great distance, "It's okay. It's probably nothing. I'll call you and tell you what they say." I still believed, somehow, that I had food poisoning.

The aide wheeled me through the big double doors while Mercy watched. I felt myself falling away from her.

THE RITUAL OF the ultrasound felt familiar, even comforting: the lumbering machine wheeled to the side of the bed, the lifted hem of my shirt, the probe in its slick coat of gel. It lasted only a few seconds. The young doctor murmured, "I'll be right back," then returned with another doctor who repeated the ultrasound and told me her findings. It all felt like something that was simply happening to me, without context or meaning. There was a discussion between the two doctors about what to do next. There was an IV, through which they threaded pain medication into my veins, dulling the cramps so that for one brief moment I could think clearly, until the soft, dizzying lift of the medicines took over. In that moment I remember thinking: *So. I'm alone again, after all.*

I lay on my side, aware of the cool spot under my cheek where my tears landed in a damp circle. They wheeled me upstairs in the gurney, which felt like floating.

EVEN THOUGH IT was Radhika's hospital, I never expected to see her there. It didn't occur to me that this was somewhere she belonged, where she could come and go without restrictions while Mercy was forced to wait outside in the cold parking lot. Later I learned that Mercy had called her. Perhaps she would have heard about me anyway, given that cases like mine fell into her specialty: how to get a dead twenty-two-week fetus out of a woman's body.

She kneeled at the side of the gurney in scrubs and a surgical mask. Above the v of her scrub top, in the depression between her clavicles, a thread of a pulse quivered, reminding me of that second heartbeat inside me, which at some point in the last few days had secretly, silently stopped.

When she left my side, I heard her hushed voice coming from the hallway, a conversation with the other doctors.

"… second trimester demise."

"… cervix closed …"

"… partner outside …"

The fact of it began to pound on my brain and my blood vessels, and I closed my eyes and tried to shut it out. *This isn't real. This isn't real. This isn't real.*

It seemed there were questions about which infection prevention protocols could be breached. The rules were, anyway, entirely new, which perhaps made them bendable, even breakable.

A nurse came back over to the gurney and told me that they were very sorry but they could not make an exception to the rules—rules that had been in existence for days, maybe hours. Mercy would not be allowed inside the hospital.

I told myself I wasn't really alone. I had Radhika. But my body yearned for Mercy. More than anything, I realized in one horrible, sickening wave, I yearned for my baby. Mercy would wait for me in the parking lot, and she would be there when I came home—to our apartment, our bed. But in the most fundamental sense I was, once again, alone. I would leave here alone.

THEY LET THE pain medication wear off just enough to allow me to have one more conversation. Radhika explained that I had a decision to make: I could be put to sleep and she could remove the baby with instruments. Or they could give me medications to induce labor.

I said I would do whatever she recommended. "There's no medical recommendation in this case, Josie. Both options are safe and effective. It's really your choice."

No, I thought. *It's not my choice. This is not my choice.*

She talked me through it again, patiently. "Some women prefer to push and deliver the baby because it feels more natural. You'll be awake, and you can hold her. If we take you to the operating room, I'll remove it in pieces. It'll be a little faster, but the main thing is that you'd be asleep. When you wake up, it'll be over. Some women feel this makes it a little easier."

Something about that word—*easier*—made me reflexively dislike this option. I said I would stay awake and deliver the baby.

I was already having contractions, they said, but they would give me medicines to make them stronger. Then they gave me more medicines "to help you forget what's happening."

The medicines made me vomit. They made my body tremble all over. But they did not make me forget what was happening. I was totally aware of what was happening. I was delivering my dead baby. Each time I let my drugged mind surface onto that conscious thought, I vomited again. *My dead baby.* Over and over.

Radhika stayed the whole time. When it finally happened—that last, terrible, emptying surge—she was the one who eased her out of my body. Then she placed her in a towel and lifted her to me.

She was tiny and beautiful. Everything about her was what I had imagined, except she didn't cry. Curled in the palm of my hand, her pale eyelids seemed to quiver, then she was still. At first her stillness was like something natural, even soothing: a placid lake, the curve of an egg. Then it became unbearable, and I let out a deep-throated wail, and I handed her back to Radhika, who took her away.

WHEN I ASKED if there was any way Mercy could hold her, the nurses conferred and returned with a solution: they would take her down to the parking lot in one of those rolling bassinets. Mercy could see her, but she wouldn't be allowed to hold her. Infection control.

They were not unkind. I saw the pain on their faces; they felt awful about all of it.

Outside the window, the afternoon looked cold and shadowed. When we'd arrived that morning, the dim night had been barely unfurling into day. Hours had passed, and now evening was falling. From where I lay propped up in the bed, blood seeping between my legs, I peered down at the parking lot thinking maybe I could see Mercy there— but the lot was enormous, the hospital vast and bulky, with many corners.

The nurses called Mercy from my phone and instructed her to wait by an unmarked door at the back of the building. Then they wheeled the baby through a quiet hallway, into an elevator, and down, down.

I've imagined it a hundred times. In the parking lot, one of the nurses lifts her out of the bassinet wrapped in a blue-and-pink blanket. She holds her up to show Mercy. In my memory that is not quite a memory, I can see Mercy in her brown coat and beanie, the accusatory look she gets whenever she's trying not to cry. She holds her face as close as she can to this tiny bundle, this daughter who is not her daughter, and she whispers a few words to her. She folds her own empty arms across her chest and rocks very slightly from side to side, as though she could tuck the small body into hers and curl over her like a mother bird, protecting her from the chill of the late afternoon. Then it's over. That's all.

They wheel her in her bassinet back to the elevator, up to the fifth floor, down the hallway to the room where I wait in my small puddle of blood.

SHE DIDN'T HAVE a name. I'd made a list, but all along I'd thought I would ask Mercy, and maybe Radhika, to help me narrow it down. Or perhaps, I'd imagined, after she was born there would be one name that fit her perfectly. In the end, when they brought the birth and death certificates for me to sign, nothing was as I imagined it. I was alone.

I chose Nivea, because she was pale and beautiful, like snow. And because by the time they brought her back to me from the parking lot, she was already cold.

21

STAYED ONE night in the hospital. From inside the dark room, through the closed door, I could hear all the new babies crying, and their mothers' gentle, delighted murmurs.

The next morning the doctors and nurses encouraged me to go home. "You'll be more comfortable there," they said. A kind nurse helped me wash the honey-thick blood from between my thighs. She told me what to do if I bled too much, or if I had pain or fever. I promised to follow all the recommendations. It seemed there was nothing else I could do.

The same nurse shuffled through a postpartum discharge bag, removing things I wouldn't need: the no-tears baby shampoo, wipes, diaper cream, tiny blue-and-pink hat. Until the only items remaining were a plastic squirt bottle and a sample pack of witch hazel pads. These were the things they gave me to take home.

They kept Nivea.

The obstetrician had recommended an autopsy. It might provide some answers, she said. I agreed to this. But it wouldn't happen until after the weekend, maybe longer. Until then, Nivea and her limp, pulseless placenta would be stored in a freezer somewhere on the Labor & Delivery floor, along with all the other dead babies. I imagined them stacked in there, the zippered bags in neat rows. Or maybe she was alone, the only tiny body in that dark box with its frosted walls, where she would remain until someone came to take her away, to be carved up and examined.

I didn't cry until they wheeled me onto the elevator and someone pressed the glowing round button. The doors drew together with their sealing, sucking finality, and the ground fell away, drawing me down, down, away from her. I could feel the tug of her body on mine, as though the elevator cables were wrenching us apart, the line that tethered us fraying and snapping—gone. I let out a wild, hollow sob that sounded like it came from someone or something else. The nurse pushing the wheelchair placed a hand on my shoulder for the briefest moment before withdrawing it again. I thought I heard her stifle a sob, but I drowned it out with my own cries, echoing against the metal walls of the elevator and through the empty, high-ceilinged lobby. They wheeled me through the glass doors to the parking lot. I looked around for Mercy, but she wasn't there. Instead, there was Radhika in her green scrubs and black vest, the wind whipping her hair into her face. Her sharp cheekbones, her searching eyes. "Josie," she said. She wrapped her arms around me and held me like a child, right there in the windblown parking lot. I smelled her clothes, the warm skin on her neck. I thought maybe it was a dream. Maybe she had come to tell me it wasn't real, it was all a mistake. I was still pregnant and would give birth to my daughter in the summer, as I had planned. But all she said was, "I'll take you home."

PART THREE

22

IN THE DAYS and weeks after I lost Nivea, I kept thinking about a conversation I'd had several years earlier. It was at a book launch party where I ended up talking with the author's sister, whose name was Amalia. When I mentioned that her sister and I were grad school classmates, she said, "Ah. You get paid to tell stories, too."

"Maybe one day. I hope."

"Sure you will. You're young. How old are you?"

I told her I was thirty.

"You got kids?" I said no. She batted a hand at me. "Good. You don't want that headache." Laughing. No, really, she loved her kids, all of them.

"How many?" I asked.

"Sometimes I joke that I have three and a half." She let out a throaty chuckle. "But my kids say that's not funny." I twirled my champagne flute between my fingers. Her face turned serious. "You like a good story? I've got one for you."

It was the story of her fourth and final pregnancy. She had three daughters already. At her second-trimester ultrasound, they told her she was carrying the boy she'd been praying for. Then they told her to stay on the exam table.

"The lady doing the scan kept putting more of that jelly on my stomach, pressing harder until I thought she was going to leave bruises. She kept saying, 'I'm not the doctor. I just take the pictures.' I said to her, 'Please, just tell me, what are you seeing?' Finally she must have felt bad for me, because she said, 'Well ma'am, I'm not seeing any fingers.'" Amalia held up a closed fist to show me, rotating it like a globe. "No fingers," she said again.

"Finally the doctor came in. Two doctors. Men. There were some things wrong with the baby, they said. Cysts on the brain, something wrong with the heart. Down syndrome, maybe. Missing fingers and toes, maybe even missing limbs. They couldn't say for sure. They weren't one hundred percent certain.

"Then they left me alone with the first lady, and she said, 'So when do you want to schedule your abortion?'

"I just looked at her. Then she got all apologetic, and she said, 'I'll step out of the room. I'll come back in ten minutes.'

"I said, 'You can give me ten minutes, you can give me a week, you can give me all the time in the world. I'm not getting any abortion. I'm not killing my baby.'" Amalia paused here, seemingly for dramatic effect. "And do you know what she said? She said, 'Ma'am, it's not a baby. It's a fetus.'"

Her voice trembled as she said it. Even then, however many years later, I could tell her anger was still fresh.

She went on: "I looked at her and said, 'You don't have kids, do you?' She said, 'No ma'am.' I told her, 'I'm a mother. I've got three kids, and I've been pregnant with this one for five months. I can feel him moving inside me. I'm not killing my little boy.'

"That's when the doctor came back in. He said, 'I should've been more clear.'

"I said, 'You were perfectly clear. And let me be clear with you: I'm not getting any abortion.'"

"So what did you do?" I said.

Her face was bold and decisive. "I did what I said I would. I had my son."

Someone squeezed past us, bumping my shoulder. A splash of champagne landed on my arm. "And was he …?"

She laughed, a short, bitter laugh. "See. I knew you were going to ask that. Everyone wants to know. *What did you get? Did you get your son? Or did you get a monster?*"

I opened my mouth, but she held up a hand. "I'll tell you what I got." She pressed her lips and her palms together as though in prayer. "I got a son."

"And is he …"

"Normal?" She gave the same little laugh, and she held up her fist again. "On the ultrasound his hand looked like this. But when he came out"—she spread and rippled her fingers like a wave—"Ten fingers, ten toes. They were all there. He just needed to open his hands."

"And his brain? The cysts?"

She shrugged. "Another doctor told me later that sometimes that happens: those cysts on the brain, they can go away on their own." She pointed through the glass doors to a cluster of men standing outside around a firepit. "There he is," she said. "He's twenty years old. My beautiful, healthy son."

And he was beautiful, with his mother's dark eyes and animated mouth, the light from the flames flashing on his face.

"The doctors were wrong," she said. "They wanted me to kill him."

I said nothing. Nothing I could have said seemed adequate to the depth of this woman's bravery and fortitude.

"That's why I don't believe in abortion," Amalia said, her voice a low, tense whisper. "That's what abortion is. It's killing a baby."

23

RADHIKA DROVE ME home from the hospital and helped me carry my things upstairs. The apartment was empty. Someone had tidied up, made the bed. A vase of wildflowers stood on the kitchen counter. "Where's Mercy?" I asked.

"Oh Josie." Radhika's eyebrows pinched together. "She wanted to come. But she was very, very emotional." I realized I'd started crying again, because she handed me a tissue. "She was a wreck, actually. I told her to wait a bit, try to calm down."

I nodded. She touched her fingertips to my forehead, as though I were a sick child. Then she promised she would call soon, and she left.

I sat in the armchair and imagined I was holding my baby in my arms, the warmth of her pressing against my chest. After a moment I felt a spreading dampness. I looked down. The front of my shirt was wet.

They had told me this might happen, and how to prevent it. I didn't take their advice. I peeled off my shirt, cupped one breast in my hand, and with the pad of the other thumb pressed down, smoothing the firm, spongy tissue toward the aching center. One watery white drop blossomed on the nipple, trembled, and fell. Then another. I let the drops splatter on my lap.

The same clouds I'd watched hovering on the horizon from the delivery room now unfurled themselves over the dull water. I sat there until my breasts were sore and the nipples raw, until the sun disappeared and the ocean turned black. Just before I fell asleep, big, round raindrops began to fall from the sky.

Sometime in the night Mercy appeared. She woke me just enough to walk me to bed, where she slipped the hospital socks off my feet and tucked me under the covers and lay down next to me. I fell asleep, the memory of her presence and the rain pelting the windows like a dream. In the morning I lay there while she dressed in the cold bedroom. She said she would be back that evening.

I turned away from her, spreading my body against the empty space on the sheets.

THERE IS SOMETHING incomplete about a love that flows in one direction, toward an unknown, unseen thing. I had no memories of her. There was nothing to smell, nothing to hold in my hands. I didn't even have the bodily memory of her movements. I had not yet felt her, or wasn't sure if I had.

I had a hospital bracelet, still attached to my wrist like a hangover. I had my swollen, aching breasts. And I had the endless, unanswerable question that I now know is asked about every miscarriage and stillbirth, the same question, a kind of survivor's guilt, that is asked after a suicide: *Was it my fault?* And the attendant magical thinking: *What if I hadn't had those sips of wine? What if I'd been younger and healthier?* And the most horrible version: *What if I'd wanted her more? What if I'd never known a single moment of ambivalence, never harbored a single doubt?*

But those are questions without answers. They don't lead anywhere. They don't make a story. *I had something—or the promise of something—and then it was gone.* A very, very short story, maybe. A private and in some ways pointless story.

The real story, I think now, lies in what I had left, or what I thought I had. Radhika. Mercy. My body with its aching emptiness, and whatever chance I might have at filling it again. My unfinished book, the ending I had yet to write.

In college, when Radhika would make her brilliant assessments of our classmates' feeble short stories, she almost always framed her remarks the same way: "The author needs to make a choice." Whatever the inconsistencies in the text, whether they related to character or plot or structure, she would diagnose it exactly, and insist that the solution lay not in our well-meaning suggestions about voice and plot and backstory but in the author's willingness and ability to stop equivocating—to take the story into her own hands and deliver it to the reader with boldness and intention. "Make a choice."

AND SO, MY first day home from the hospital, I made two decisions.

I would give up the novel. I'd let it go on for too long. By trying so hard to mold and manipulate it, I'd allowed it to mutate into something I no longer recognized. I had destroyed it. It was time to let go—finally—of what I couldn't save. The same way my body had done. Maybe

I could begin again, start something new. But I was not the type of person who could write a story beginning at the end, the way Radhika could, or the way Amalia could. I could only write my way forward, making sense of one thing at a time and wrestling with my own instincts, indecision, and uncertainty.

And: I would get pregnant again, as soon as I could. This time I wouldn't let anyone else try to help me or sway me. Not Radhika. Not Mercy.

I called my doctor's office and asked to schedule a postpartum appointment. The kind receptionist asked, "When did you deliver?"

"Yesterday."

"Wonderful! Congratulations."

"The baby died," I said.

She told me she was very sorry. Then she said she could schedule me to speak with a doctor as soon as that afternoon, if I'd like. "Currently all visits are by phone or video, except for those requiring an urgent exam."

I said that would be fine.

On my phone there was a text from Eleanor.

Eleanor: u staying safe, Josie?

me: yes. Sheltering in place, like a good citizen.

Eleanor: don't want to say I told you so. but.

me: ha.

Eleanor: it can't be easy to dealing with all this while ur pregnant.

me: I'm not pregnant anymore, actually. I lost it.

Eleanor: oh god, josie. I'm sorry. R u ok?

me: I think so. I'm sad.

Eleanor: what do u need?

me: I think I just need to be alone for a while.
Eleanor: well. Ur on the right planet, then.

IT RAINED ALL morning, gray water running in the streets and swirling in the drains. On my laptop I scrolled through headlines about a cruise ship in the Port of Oakland, bodies piling up in the streets in Italy. I felt as though the world and its concerns were unfolding alongside my own life in a separate, parallel universe.

I closed the browser. Then I opened the email from Sarah Marshall that Radhika had forwarded to me. I copied her email address into a new window and wrote to her. I said that I was very sorry to have kept her waiting, but I'd decided not to complete the manuscript after all.

I no longer plan to publish this or any novel. I plan to start a family, which I anticipate will take most of my time and energy. I genuinely appreciate the thought and care you put into reading my work.

My hands trembled as I typed, not with fear, but with a kind of terrible certainty. I didn't expect a response, but a few minutes later there was a message in my inbox:

Dear Josie,
Thanks for letting me know about your book project. I've thought more than once over the past few months about the partial manuscript Radhika sent me. Sad to think of it never getting out into the world ... You're certainly a gifted writer. But I can hardly blame you for wanting to stay out of the commercial publishing fray.

Motherhood seems like a very worthwhile endeavor—
though I wouldn't know from personal experience.
I wish you all the best.
Sarah M.

I read the message several times. Then I closed my computer and put it on the floor. Placing my hands over the smooth, scaphoid space below my navel, I let myself feel its new emptiness, the sorrow and hope that dwelled there.

THE DOCTOR WHO called was one I'd never met before. She was polite and professional. She asked about my bleeding. I told her it was light.

"And your pain?"

"I don't have any pain."

She told me she was very sorry about the loss of my pregnancy, and I thanked her.

"What else can I help you with today, Josie?"

I asked her when I could try to get pregnant again. She paused. "Generally we advise three months. In your case, because you were in the second trimester, I might advise waiting a little longer."

"Is that an evidence-based recommendation?" I asked, plucking from memory a phrase I'd heard from Radhika.

After a beat she said, "I don't know that there is precise evidence behind it." Then she added, "But from your chart I see that you were a fertility patient. Is that right?"

I told her it was.

"So, I imagine you'll be waiting several months anyway." I waited for her to go on. I could tell she was tired of saying the same things over and over, repeating what was to her, by now, obvious. But I needed her to spell it out for me. "All the fertility clinics are closed. Everything is on hold until there's better … control."

I squeezed my eyes shut until the black swam with white and red shapes. "How long?"

"We don't know," she said.

I MIGHT'VE REVISITED my decision to abandon the novel, since I had, for the moment, no other ambition to pursue—at least as long as the fertility clinic remained closed. Instead I doubled down. It was never the point, I reasoned, to choose one or the other, the baby or the book. The point was to stop trying to prove anything, to anyone. I would live my life on my own, as I knew how to do, as I'd done before Radhika reappeared, and before Mercy showed up with her wide eyes and her innocent promises.

When Mercy returned that evening, she took a long time pulling off her boots. I could feel her watching me from the doorway, and I felt suddenly annoyed with her, standing there in her socks, jacket dripping, wet curls plastered against her face. "Josie?"

I said nothing. The rain had slowed to a near-silent drip-drip outside the window. In the faintest distance, the ocean purred its slow, muffled rhythm. After a moment she stepped toward me. I shook my head slightly, as though to warn her off. I thought we both might dissolve into a million miserable pieces, two piles of dust on the floor.

"Can I hold you?" she said finally, her voice choking. "I just really want to hold you."

I didn't say no. She crossed the room and sank to her knees, wrapping her arms around me. I didn't move. She put her head in my lap. We were both crying, and I felt the saddest and the coldest feeling I'd ever felt in my life. I felt how much we had both loved Nivea, and at the same time I felt that no one could—or would—love any child of mine as much as I would. It was a promise I made to myself. Mercy might even have called it an ambition. I wrapped my heart around it.

24

THE VERY NEXT day Radhika called with her own news: she was taking a leave of absence from the hospital. "There are plenty of other doctors who can do the same work I do. And the chance of exposure at the hospital is so high. It's not worth the risk to the kids."

"Is there a risk for you, too?" I said. "Your health, I mean?"

She sniffed. "What about my health? I'm not a chemo patient anymore."

I felt silly for bringing it up. What did I know about these things? "It'll give you more time to write," I said.

"Exactly."

Within a week, however, her pragmatic optimism had turned to dark frustration. Her voice was strained and rattled on the phone. "What was I thinking, imagining I could possibly get any writing done in this house?"

"Isn't Mercy with the kids?"

"Mercy is a saint. But no single adult can keep two kids occupied indoors for ten hours a day. They're down in my office constantly. *Mama I'm bored. Mama when are you going to stop working?*" she whined in Saniya's voice. "Meanwhile Adam's locked away in a closet on his super important Zoom meetings, doing his super important job. Nobody bothers *him*. It's just me, me. *Mama, Mama.*"

"Oh Rad, I'm sorry."

She breathed a shuddering sigh. "I keep telling myself this will all be over in six weeks. That's the only way I can get through it. Then it'll be summer, and the kids can go to camp, and I can go back to work. It'll all go back to normal."

"I hope that's how it is," I said, thinking of the fertility clinic. I could've told her my big decision—that I'd finally let go of the novel, that I was determined to become pregnant again. She might've been proud of me for it. But something held me back. Maybe I sensed or feared some judgment from her, where Sarah Marshall had offered pure endorsement. *A very worthwhile endeavor.* So I just said, "I want it to go back to normal, too. I miss you."

"Ah, Josie," she sighed. "I miss you too. We all do. And I do want to find a way to see each other, once it's safe."

MEANWHILE, MERCY KEPT appearing in my doorway every night after she'd put the twins to bed. She brought me groceries, soup she'd cooked in Radhika's kitchen, her grandmother's tamales. We sat six feet apart. I picked at my food. Leftovers piled up in my fridge.

"Does Rad know you're here?" I asked her.

"She knows. She doesn't like it. But she can't stop me from coming."

"Can't she?"

"I told her I would quit if I couldn't see you."

I thought about this for a moment. "And what about your family? Does she know you go there, too?" Myra was still hosting Sunday dinners at her house with their parents, aunts, uncles, and cousins. Even Mercy's grandmother came, with her weak heart and swollen ankles.

"Radhika knows everything," Mercy said. "She just doesn't want to let you know she knows."

"What's the point of that?"

Mercy just shrugged.

The strained distance between us was palpable, despite Mercy's dogged loyalty—maybe because of it. Sometimes we talked about Nivea, and we cried together. Then I could see, always as though I were realizing it for the first time, how genuinely Mercy had loved her, how in some ways Nivea had been even more real to her than she was to me.

I WENT "BACK to work," meaning the symphony shipped me my laptop and informed me I would be pivoting to managing web content while the season was on indefinite hiatus. And so I had something to occupy my time. But I longed for the muffled sounds of the orchestra tuning, my colleagues' quiet coughs and shuffling papers across the cubicle dividers, the pipes creaking behind the walls.

I texted Eleanor every few days to see how she was holding up.

Eleanor: I'm fine. My anxiety is thru the roof but it helps that I don't have to leave the house. how bout u? mercy taking good care of u?

me: Mercy comes over. But she still lives at Radhika's house.
Eleanor: um ... why??? I thought R stopped working?
Eleanor: what's going on with u guys?
me: nothing. Rad needs her help more than I do, that's all.

"Are things getting any better?" I asked Radhika on the phone one afternoon. It had finally stopped raining. I was watching a bird on a telephone wire, its tiny head tilting to one side, then the other.

"Not really. It's impossible to concentrate in this house. The whining, the demands." She blew out a breath. "Who knows what's going to happen—if we'll even go to Chicago this summer, if the kids will start kindergarten. I asked my publisher for an extension on my deadline. Or Sarah Marshall asked for me."

"Did she get it?"

"She did. Apparently all publishing timelines are out the window, anyway. I'm sure my pub date is the least of anyone's concerns."

"I doubt that's true," I said, trying to lift her spirits. "And even if it is, then great. Use the time to your advantage."

She hesitated. I sensed that she wanted to contradict me, but she seemed to swallow the words. "Thanks, Josie." I braced myself for what I knew she was going to say next. "What about you? Have you been working on the ending?"

I'd rehearsed exactly how I would answer this question. But I heard myself say, "Not as much as I'd meant to. It's only been a few weeks, you know, since ..." Playing for her sympathy, like a coward.

"Oh, Josie. I know." Her voice was tender. "But you'll get back to it when you're ready. I know you will. You're so much closer than you think."

THE TRUTH IS that I was writing. I'd started the very next day after returning from the hospital, the day of my two big decisions. Instead of the novel, I wrote about whatever was on my mind, whatever was happening—which wasn't much. I wrote about Radhika and Mercy and my dreams of Nivea, and the sky over the ocean through my living room window, and the inscrutable masked faces on my long walks on the beach. I wrote memories from my childhood, some of which were returning to me for the first time. I filled pages and pages in my spiral notebooks.

I suppose it was a diary. That's what it was.

25

I WAS HARDLY surprised when Mercy caught the virus. They all got it: Myra, Myra's daughters, Daniela and Steve, a couple of aunts and uncles. Only Mercy's grandmother somehow managed to avoid it.

"Did Myra bring it home from the ER?"

"We don't know. None of the other nurses got it. No one's sure where it came from."

"Well, the important thing is that you're all okay."

"We are," she said. Then, after a beat, "Radhika's pissed, though. She banished me to Myra's house."

"For how long?"

"Two weeks of quarantine, at least. But she hasn't said if I can go back after that."

"Jeez. She must be mad."

"Furious." There was a pause. Then she said: "What about you? Are you going to be okay on your own for two weeks?"

"Of course," I said, holding the phone slightly away from my face. "Of course I'll be okay."

INTERMINABLE GRAY APRIL bled into May. Rain and dripping milk, tender green on the trees. Without Mercy's visits my days lost all semblance of structure. I stayed up too late reading, then slept late, dragging myself out of bed at noon, blinking in the midmorning light. Reading copy for the symphony website, I found my own mistakes scattered like weeds—stuff I never would've missed before. The mostly empty fridge started to smell sour. Most nights I ate pasta without sauce.

The truth was I wasn't okay. Not really.

I was angry at Mercy. She had been reckless; she'd endangered Radhika's children, and, just as egregiously, she'd destroyed the fine balance of Radhika's time, her family, her writing. Now each of us was alone—or at least Radhika and I were—and it was Mercy's fault.

But it was Radhika's fault, too, in a way. As I wrote—in the evenings and late into the night, scribbling in my diary, my hand aching—I began to see, as perhaps I had vaguely seen in those days before I lost Nivea, my sort of pathetic attachment to Radhika. She had seemed so different from other women I knew: a mother who insisted on her own creative and intellectual life, who would prioritize adult conversation and collaboration over baths and bedtime stories. But when tested, she had ultimately chosen her family, her children, over our friendship. I couldn't really fault her. Of course she had to protect them. But I hated that she'd seen me, all along, as a risk. "When it's safe," she said. But who would determine what "safe" meant, and when? Radhika would.

I texted her, hoping to get her version of the story, to hear her righteous judgment of Mercy and take some kind of comfort in it. I thought she might need some comforting, too. I imagined her spiraling, suffocating in that house with her kids, no one there to help her.

She didn't text back.

AND THEN TWO things happened in the final days of Mercy's quarantine, both of them totally unplanned—although I suppose I have to take responsibility.

The first was that I went to Aquatic Park. It was a place my dad had talked about when I was a kid, where you could jump straight from the San Francisco streets into the cold, shimmering bay. "No wet suits allowed," I remembered him telling me with a raised eyebrow, like a challenge.

In my years in the city I'd heard other swimmers talk about it; I'd even gone by there once or twice, peering around the side of the white clapboard building with its weathered sign: The Dolphin Club. Watching the swimmers dip and disappear into the icy bay as though it were the most natural and comfortable thing in the world, smiling and splashing like Labradors.

In the years since my parents died I hadn't once stood on a mountain, hiked anything but a paved trail, or swum in the open water. But one afternoon during those long, lonely weeks I pulled my bike out of storage and dusted off the handlebars. I guess I was desperate to swim, anywhere, any way that I could.

The door to the Dolphin Club building was closed and padlocked. But I noticed a few men and women, white-haired and tanned to a wrinkled sheen, ambling in and out of a gap in the gate, which was barely secured with a loose chain. They carried towels and goggles; some swung large, empty paint buckets by their handles. Around the side of the building I could make out one or two swimmers in the open water.

I guess I'd been there a while, perched on my bike with one leg stuck out like a kickstand. I heard a woman's voice ask: "Here to swim?"

She had blue eyes and white hair that framed a wide, smiling face, two towels and pair of orange flippers under one arm, a giant thermos in the other.

My voice caught briefly in my throat. "Not today."

"Ah. But you're a swimmer." She tilted her head, looking at me as though she'd known me all my life.

"My usual pool is closed."

"'Course it is. Well, I think technically this place is closed, too. But we keep coming. And I guess Public Health sort of looks the other way, because, you know, what are they going to say?" She gave a little laugh and another shrug. "It's social distancing, right?"

I heard myself answer as though I'd thought this all out very clearly. "I've always thought that's the wonderful thing about swimming: you can be alone and with other people at the same time. At my old pool, I didn't really know anyone, but it still felt like kind of a community. And then, once you're underwater"—I lifted a hand off the handlebars, suddenly expansive—"you're totally alone. You don't have to talk to anyone." I don't know what got into me. It had been days since I'd seen another human or said actual words out loud.

But she was right there with me. "The best of both worlds. I completely agree." Then she laughed again, like she'd just realized the most hilarious thing. "I don't even know you! I'm Carol."

I told her my name and she didn't miss a beat. "Have you done any open water swimming before, Josie?" She seemed to have already decided she liked me, or at least trusted me.

I glanced at the water. "I used to swim in lakes and the ocean with my dad. When I was a kid."

"Well, come back here any weekday at three with your suit and cap. I'm happy to sneak—ahem, *bring* you in. As my guest." She winked at me. "If you're not scared off by the cold."

As I biked home, panting hard on the hills, I thought about Carol and what she'd offered me, the strange world I'd glimpsed at the city's edge, between the land and the freezing, terrifying water. I thought about my parents and their lonely deaths. I wondered if I would ever go back.

BEFORE I HAD time to think much more about it (by then it was the last day of Mercy's quarantine—I was counting), something else happened, something I'm still ashamed of. I went to Radhika's house.

I wasn't hoping or expecting to see her. She'd told me they were going to get out that day: a walk along the Golden Gate Bridge, or a picnic at Alta Plaza, I can't remember, and it didn't matter. She'd given me the distinct impression they would be gone. There were other impressions, too, including that she and Adam sometimes left the back door unlocked, and that they almost never set the house alarm.

Still, it took some boldness on my part. I'd barely left my apartment in two months. When I set off on my bike that shimmering spring morning, for the second time in two days, my pulse was pounding in my ears.

If I didn't want to see her, then what did I want? I suppose I wanted simply to be near to her. Also—I can admit this now—I wanted answers. I heard the growing desperation in her voice when she talked about her children, and I remembered a story she'd written in college, one that had stirred a fierce discussion in our fiction workshop. It was about a mother who mercilessly, repeatedly, beat her small children. Our classmates had called the main character intolerably cruel, the story's violence heinous and gratuitous. I'd actually thought the story, though difficult to read, was one of Radhika's best—certainly better than most of our classmates' work. It had seemed to me that they used the brutality of the story's main character to rationalize their petty dislike of the author, though I didn't say this out loud. It didn't matter. She didn't need my defense.

But now, I couldn't help it: her story came back to me, and I suspected her of keeping some dark secret. Although what kind of evidence or corroboration I expected to discover in that house, I really can't say.

IT HAD BEEN six weeks since I'd been there. Standing alone in her kitchen, barely breathing, it all came rushing back: The way the sun beamed through the skylights. The big wooden table that always seemed as if it would give off splinters but never did. A bowl of ripe fruit, a fistful of daffodils stuck in a mason jar, a stack of overdue library books on the counter. What it felt like to be in her field of energy, her radiating generosity, the infectious intentionality and purpose in everything she did.

It was eerie, almost chilling, to be there without her.

I looked around, trying my best to be purposeful. Nearly every moment I'd spent in that house had been in the kitchen. I'd never been upstairs: the sanctum, the place where only the family—and once, in the not-so-distant past, Mercy—was allowed.

The wooden stairs creaked under my footsteps. At the top of the landing, Adam's office (swiveling leather chair, paired flat screens), a bathroom, and the kids' room: canary yellow carpet, tulip curtains, a scattered box of magnet tiles, picture books strewn across every surface. Their room contained more traces of Radhika than I'd expected. A photo of her with Saniya and Sachin framed on the dresser. A picture book with the title *Sex Is a Funny Word*, undoubtedly her educational addition to their little library. A pair of her running socks, well-known to me from her toes curled over the edge of my chair, balled up next to the hamper.

After lingering in the doorway, I tiptoed down the hall to the master bedroom but found myself utterly uninterested in trespassing there. Whatever mysteries Radhika contained, I was certain the answers didn't lie in her and Adam's unmade bed, their spilling dresser drawers.

Downstairs, then. Not the kitchen, but farther down, to her basement office. The door off the garage, across from Mercy's room, the same one I'd found locked on Boxing Day. It was now slightly ajar. I nudged it with the toe of my sneaker. It swung open easily.

And there it was: the hidden thing, Radhika's office—if not exactly a secret, then a revelation. I could not have been more surprised if it had contained burners of bubbling potions and jars of pickled brains. It was a windowless rectangular room, its walls covered, from floor to ceiling, with images of her children. Pictures of them at every age—actual photographs, the kind you have to pick up from Walgreens, printed on shiny, five-by-seven-inch rectangles: Saniya and Sachin as newborns, swaddled in baby blankets or nuzzled by grandparents. As toddlers on park slides, splashing in a kiddie pool, sitting on Santa's knee. The two of them in their plastic bassinets—the same photo I'd seen framed in the Christmas ornament, the one Radhika had called "gross." Here it hung in a place of honor, blown up to nearly poster size, among hundreds of other photos of the twins in the hospital and in their earliest days at home: nursing on the couch, one at a time, always on Radhika's right breast, the brown gash of a scar visible on the left. Radhika bent over, beaming, cupping each little body in the crook of her elbow. The brown edge of her single nipple. The red rims of her eyes.

There was no obvious order to the display. Rather, the impression was of disorder, and of excess. There wasn't a single bare centimeter on those plastered walls. Some photos were pinned on top of one another, two or three layers thick. Mixed in among them were the kids' artistic creations. All the trite construction paper projects that adorned the kitchen, which I'd always assumed were rotated to the recycling bin every few weeks. Not so. This was their final destination. There were Valentine's hearts and candy canes and cotton-ball bearded Santa Clauses. Some pieces I recognized; dozens, possibly hundreds more I'd never seen, dating back to the kids' earliest scribbles. One appeared to be a fingerpainting executed on the inside of a plastic yogurt lid.

There were, unsurprisingly, shelves stuffed with books, and a desk with Radhika's laptop squared neatly in the center. Next to it lay a few printed pages; I recognized some of them as short segments of her book—the few bits she'd shown me. I could see my handwriting scattered between the double-spaced lines, and, in her red ink, some of her own notes. *Agree. Cut. Bring this out more.* Clearly she got some writing done in this room. But how, I couldn't imagine. It was like a shrine, a monument to the children whom she so deliberately kept at arm's length, especially, most stringently, while she worked.

As my gaze floated over the desk, something caught my eye. It was a photo, but a different kind of photo than the ones stuck to the walls. This one was small, square, black-and-white, and printed on flimsier, glossier paper. I stepped forward, peering more closely. I recognized it immediately. It was mine.

After that very first prenatal appointment, I'd headed to the pool and then straight to Radhika's house, bearing my shiny strip of black-and-white photos. How she'd gazed at them, and at me, her eyes gleaming with love and something that I took to be pride.

Who gives a friend an ultrasound photo of their six-week embryo? But I'd had no one else to give it to. I'd taken a pair of kitchen scissors from the knife block on the counter and, from the strip of six, sliced straight through the white border, handing her the bottom image. At the time I'd wanted nothing more than for her to have it. But now I wanted it back. I suppose even then I could sense her pulling away from me. Before she got too far, I wanted to reclaim what was mine. Especially—fiercely—every scrap of anything having to do with Nivea.

I snatched the photo from the desk, and as I did, a few papers beneath it drifted to the floor. Just as I was reaching to pick them up, I heard a door slam. From above, the kids' voices, their rapid footsteps crossing the kitchen. I whirled around. Behind me, directly across from the door to the garage, was a second door. I darted to it, flipped the inner latch, turned the handle. The door didn't budge. I leaned my shoulder into it. This time, with a scrape and a sucking sound, it opened, and I was blinking in the cloud-dappled afternoon, in the side alley where my bike leaned against a lamppost. I fumbled with the lock, flung my leg over the crossbar and pedaled away, breathing hard, the shiny square photo shoved in my back pocket.

26

THE NEXT DAY was the first of May. The end of Mercy's quarantine. She called first thing in the morning. I was sitting cross-legged on the bed, folding laundry. She sounded breathless. "I'm going back to Radhika's house."

In the background I could hear snatches of recorded music, the Vivaldi Double Cello Concerto. "When?"

"Today."

"Today?" In my residual, guilty adrenaline rush from the previous day I wondered for a desperate moment if Radhika had discovered something, if she was bringing Mercy over to show her the fresh, damning evidence of my crime.

"I guess she's pretty desperate for the help. And she considers me 'safe,' now that I've had the virus."

I burned with some mix of jealousy and disappointment and fear. "Great," I said. "I'm glad she came around."

In the background the music faded as she paced the first floor of Myra's house. "It's better than that, actually. I get to set the terms."

"What terms?"

"You."

I smoothed a dish towel across my knees, waiting for her to explain.

"She knows I want to keep seeing you. I figured she wants to see you, too. I proposed that you and I could visit outside every evening, on her porch, wearing masks, sitting six feet apart. And if she feels safe, she could even see you, too. I can watch the kids an extra hour or two in the evenings, and you guys can start your writing sessions again." I heard the triumph in her voice. She was delighted with herself.

I felt frantic, at once dismayed and hopeful. "And she agreed to it?"

"I actually think I convinced her that it would be good for everyone. Including her."

"Wow. Thanks." Even as I said it, I felt my own subtle deceitfulness. I knew I should be grateful to Mercy for sticking her neck out for me. But I felt crushed by the thought that she'd had to twist Radhika's arm. I was also terrified of returning there after what I'd done.

She must have sensed my hesitation because she said, "I know how much you miss her."

"I do." I stared at a crumpled pile of underwear. "And I miss you, too."

"Me too." I heard the zip of her duffel bag closing. "So. I'll see you tonight then?"

"Tonight?"

"Yeah. I'm heading there now to spend the day with the kids. Rad said you could come anytime after six."

"Okay," I said. "I'll be there."

I TOOK THE same route I'd ridden the day before to Radhika's house, wheeled my bike through the side gate and leaned it against the porch railing.

I knew it would be different meeting on the porch rather than at the kitchen table, masks on, six feet between us, the obvious and unspoken absences: she was no longer working. I was no longer pregnant and—the thing she still didn't know—no longer writing the novel. I would tell her tonight, as soon as I saw her.

What I couldn't have imagined was the difference in Radhika. She was like a shell of herself, her facial bones even more prominent, cheeks sunken under shadowed eyes. I could see the outline of her ribs through her sweater, and at the hollow base of her throat, that quivering pulse I'd noticed in the hospital, like a caged bird flapping its wings. Her voice, usually so calm and confident, was hoarse. When she sat down across from me, she seemed to collapse into the teak chair. I felt nothing but pity for her, even though the thing draining her—motherhood—was exactly the thing I wanted for myself.

"Oh Rad," I said, trying to mask my concern, "it's so good to be here. I've missed you."

"I missed you too, Josie. I'm sorry it's been so long."

"I can only imagine how hard this all is on you." I wondered if she could see it or smell it on me, my act of betrayal.

She shook her head. Her hair was trimmed close to her head, leaving her tiny ears exposed. She'd been cutting it herself with Adam's clippers. "It's not so bad. Adam and I are so lucky—blessed, really. I can't complain."

"You can complain to me."

"Thanks." She smiled weakly. "I do kind of feel like screaming sometimes." She glanced toward the French doors, her eyes wide and terribly sad. "I want so much to protect them. And then they drive me batshit crazy." From an upstairs window I could hear Saniya instructing Sachin and Mercy in the details of some game. Radhika sighed, leaning back in her chair. "But I'm glad Mercy convinced me to do this. I think I needed someone to push me out of my comfort zone, to start seeing people again."

I said, "I'm glad she convinced you, too."

Then she glanced toward the house and said in a low, gravely voice, "Someone was here, you know."

My throat and fingers tingled. I forced myself to look at her. "Where?"

"In the house." She gestured through the window. "Yesterday, while we were out."

"How do you know?"

She shrugged, almost too nonchalantly. "Some papers in my office were shuffled around."

I had the sense that she was feigning calm, barely managing to contain something inside her—rage, or perhaps fear. "Was anything missing?"

She blinked. "Nothing valuable. Adam says if anyone had actually gone through the trouble to break in, they would've taken something." She gestured again toward the house as though to indicate all their desirable possessions, ripe for the picking. "But I'm sure someone was here. Maybe it wasn't a break-in. Maybe I forgot to lock the door. It's possible. I've been pretty distracted lately." Images flashed through my mind of a police investigation, fingerprints, DNA samples. "They must've left through my office door," she was saying. "It was partly open when we got back. Just barely. I always keep it locked from the inside."

"Gosh, Rad, I'm sorry." The crazy thing is that I actually felt bad for her. She looked so small and vulnerable, her bony shoulders hunched over her long torso, elbows all pointy and ashy. "Even if nothing was missing. Just that feeling of someone being in your house, touching your things. It's so—"

"Violating," she said, cutting me off.

I glanced at her. She looked straight back at me. "Yes. Exactly." And in that moment, despite or even because of my cruel deception, I felt our prior closeness returning. As though I had strengthened a bond between us by, as she put it, violating her. The late sun filtered through the slats of the fence, and for a moment the whole backyard felt sacred and protected, like a bowl of light. A few birds tittered and chirped over our heads. She sighed and glanced wearily at her laptop, which sat closed on the table between us. "Anyway, I managed to write a few pages today, which is more than I've done in weeks." She tapped her fingers on the table. "But I'm excited to see *your* progress."

I took a breath. "Well, I didn't bring anything from the novel." I pulled a loose stack of typed pages from my backpack.

She wrinkled her eyebrows. "What's this?"

That afternoon, as I'd prepared to return to Radhika's house, I'd suddenly realized I couldn't arrive empty-handed. If it wasn't going to be the novel, I had to have something to bring her, something to show for myself. So I'd thumbed through my notebooks, reading over what I'd written during the weeks since Nivea's birth and death. I chose a few pages of loose thoughts, memories, things that had bubbled to the surface over those long, lonely days while the milk dried in my body and the winter sunlight traced its path across the living room floor. I'd typed them up and printed them out, stuffed them into my backpack without letting myself read them again. Now she held them in her hands. "I've been doing some writing by hand. Stream of consciousness, I guess you could call it."

"For what?"

"Just for me, I guess, for now."

She was flipping through the pages, looking confused. "You want me to critique this?"

My lungs felt tight under my ribs. "Not necessarily. I'm just interested in what you think."

"Okay, sure." She put the pages down. "But where are you with the novel? Do you think you'll have something to send to Sarah Marshall soon?"

After all my intentions and preparations, I fell back on a lie. "Yes! I'll bring something from the novel next time." And almost without knowing what I was doing, I reached across the table and slid the typed pages back toward me, into my backpack. Radhika didn't say anything. She hardly seemed to notice.

IN CONTRAST TO Radhika, Mercy, when she appeared, looked healthier than ever, her cheeks flushed in the final rays of the evening sun. "God, it's good to see you," she said, crossing an ankle over the opposite knee, beaming at me from the other side of the table.

It was true. It was a relief, especially after my tense hour with Radhika, to be in Mercy's company. I had missed her. I could almost admit this to myself.

"I think this is going to be good for everyone," she said. "Especially for Rad."

"She looks really stressed."

She nodded. "I never used to think of her as the anxious type, you know?"

I held my wrist in my hand. "Do you think it's anxiety about the virus? Or is it something else?"

"Honestly, I think she's mostly exhausted. And bored out of her mind. It's not like Rad is one of those moms who loves hanging out with her kids all day."

Once again I felt sorry for Radhika, almost defensive.

"And that's fine," Mercy said with a little laugh. "That's what I'm here for."

BACK AT HOME that night, exhausted from the long bike ride, I pulled the crumpled pages out of my backpack and read them once again.

What could I have been thinking, forcing them on Radhika? This wasn't a story. It was the diary of a little girl. It was me writing in my notebook on the floor, over the muffled sounds of the piano and the clicking of a computer keyboard below. The irascible, restrained ambition of two academics raising an only child. The neatly drawn boundaries. The hikes in the stoic mountains, the trail lunches of dry bread and sweating cheese. My utterly normal, claustrophobic yearning to break free of it all—interrupted by their swift, incomprehensible deaths.

I cried as I read them, out of some mix of self-pity and disgust and relief. I threw the pages in the trash and went to bed, where I tried not to think, or remember, or imagine.

BUT I DID remember. It didn't matter how hard I tried. I didn't so much see their faces or hear their voices as I felt them in my bones.

Lying on my stomach in my bedroom while they worked downstairs. Reading or writing, propped on my elbows, the skin rubbed raw by the carpet. The neighborhood sounds out the window: a car passing, squirrels chattering, the brush of tree leaves against the slanted roof. The faint whistle of the draft under the doorway.

When they died I knew what was expected of me: self-sufficiency, self-reliance. The ability to be alone. They had trained me for it, though perhaps not with this particular circumstance in mind.

Every summer for as long as I could remember, they had taken me on family backpacking trips: each person carries their own pack. Even if you're ten years old. That was the rule. That was fairness, respect, decency. To ask someone else—even your mother or father—to carry your share was to be a burden, unwelcome.

When I was fourteen and started bleeding, I never told my mother. There was no reason to tell her. Sometime in the preceding year our bathroom cabinet had been silently stocked with menstrual pads. One small box each of "light" and "heavy," in pink and purple packaging— enough to get me started when I needed them. She must have bought those pads just for me. She would've been in her midfifties by then, done with menopause. But I didn't understand that at the time. What I knew was that just as silently as the pads had appeared, I was to accept them and make use of them.

By summer I had bled three or four times, heavily and unpredictably. In July my parents planned a weeklong backpacking trip in the Sierra foothills. For the first two days I was grumpy, ornery, uncooperative. On the third day I started to bleed, heavier than I'd ever bled before, and with throbbing cramps. My lower back ached under the weight of my pack, and my legs felt tingly and weak. With every step I could feel blood oozing out of me.

"I have to pee again," I said, and I could see my father's consternation in the line of his mouth. Crouching behind a boulder, I peeled the blood-soaked pad from between my legs, used another pad to mop up the stain on my pants, chucked them both into a bush, rummaged for yet another in my pack. I could feel my father's impatience crackling from the trail, where he and my mother stood waiting for me, never putting down their packs. *What is she doing back there? How many times can one girl pee in an hour?*

I burned with adolescent resentment. Especially for her, with her stupid hand that must have made everything harder—typing, teaching, hiking, camping. She never complained, hardly acknowledged it, even though the stumps of her severed fingers glowed red and swollen in the heat. Whenever we stopped at a creek I would see her soak them silently, briefly, in the cold water.

Waiting for me that day on the trail, she would have placated him, quietly and ineffectively, and only until he began to yell. By the time I emerged from behind the rock, my thighs still sticky with blood, a sweatshirt tied around my waist, she was silent. Not because she was scared of his anger, but because that was always her approach to my dad and our bitter fights. I suppose it was another way she taught me to take care of myself.

I fought back, yelled back at him, refused to keep going.

I was fourteen. Of course I lost.

Their next trip was at the end of that summer, one week before the start of the ninth grade. I stayed behind, made arrangements to stay with a friend. My dad said that was fine; he didn't try to persuade me to come along, and neither did she. That was the trip where they were struck by a cascade of falling rocks and knocked off the edge of the mountain, falling to their deaths. Alone.

I still think about my mom's hand, how it might have—must have—kept her from grabbing on when and where she needed to. Just like that doctor had tried to tell her, all those years ago.

27

THE NEXT AFTERNOON I rode to the Dolphin Club, a towel rolled in my backpack, a swimsuit under my clothes, arriving a few minutes before three o'clock. Carol was waiting for me by the gate.

The first time we waded in together she held my hand like a child. I felt afraid, though of what I wasn't sure. I didn't know why I'd come, or what I hoped for. Maybe I was afraid that whatever I was looking for, I wouldn't find it here.

When the water reached our hips Carol let go of my hand and pushed off, gliding a few yards ahead of me. She wore bright orange fins and an orange cap, making her easy to spot in the dark water. "Keep your eyes on me," she said. "Don't worry about where we are, just stay close. I won't lose you." Then she ducked her head under, and I followed.

The cold wrapped itself around my chest, squeezing me like a fist. We swam for a minute or two—I had no idea how far or for how long. Like Carol said, I didn't focus on where we were, couldn't focus on anything but the cold, every hair follicle on my body prickling. It reminded me of being pregnant, and for a moment I fought back a surge of nausea. I had the urge to grab for something—a hand to hold onto. I thought of Mercy. Then Carol stopped and lifted her head, and I did the same. "How do you feel?" she asked.

"Cold."

She beamed. "We'll warm up after a few hundred yards. You're doing great."

Back underwater, I followed the orange blur of Carol's fins, and every time I lifted my head over the sloshing surface I looked for her orange cap. The grip of the cold on my body gradually loosened. In the distance, the Golden Gate Bridge loomed over us like an anchor dropped from the sky.

MY PERIOD RETURNED. One morning it was just there, like an old friend, a reminder of what my body was capable of—no penis required. Only the nurse practitioner with her long syringe.

Suddenly life was busy again, the days getting longer, stretching toward summer. A new routine: I rose early to the first hints of sunrise. Coffee, ten or twelve handwritten pages in my notebook—whatever was on my mind, whatever was happening. I pushed aside the embarrassment I'd felt on rereading the pages I'd brought to Radhika's house. As long as I didn't show it to anyone, keeping a diary was perfectly fine. I enjoyed it, and I had nothing else to be working on, so why not continue?

Then the symphony workday at my desk, double- and triple-checking my copy, followed by a late lunch and a long bike ride to meet Carol at the Dolphin Club. After that first day, I came with the same supplies as Carol: two towels, a thermos filled with hot water, a pair of warm socks. "Since the showers and sauna are closed," she explained, "we have to improvise."

Also that day Carol gave me an old wet suit top to wear over my swimsuit. I looked around. "No one else is wearing one."

"Don't worry about anyone else," she said.

Every day I followed Carol out into the bay, the solid bridge in the distance, the crisp, sloshing line where the water met the sky, less than an inch from my nose and as far as I could see. "When it feels too choppy or too scary, that's when you need to take a break," Carol said, treading water in her orange flippers. "Stop trying to get anywhere. Just float along for a while. Clinging to the water, trying to grab onto it—that's how people drown. Let it hold you."

I got used to that: floating on my back with Carol, staring at the sky, feeling the rise and fall of my chest, my lungs filling with air, lifting me like a buoy.

And I got used to what Carol called "warming ourselves from the inside out" afterward: changing out of our wet swimsuits, sitting on benches with our hair wrapped in towels, our feet stuck in paint buckets of steaming water, drinking hot tea.

It turned out Carol had lost a child, too. Her only son, Christopher, had been run over by a school bus when he was six years old. "I still celebrate his birthday," she told me. "He would be forty-two this October."

We talked over the lapping sounds of the bay stroking the shore. I told her about Nivea, a little about Mercy. Sometimes we said nothing at all.

And then back on my bike, to Radhika's house. Like the previous winter and spring, I arrived with my ponytail dripping, goggle rings around my eyes—only now instead of smelling of chlorine I smelled of bay water, the city air that blew in my face on my uphill ride to Laurel Heights, the herbal tea bags that Carol always packed for us. I let myself in through the side gate, parked my bike in the yard and waited for her on the porch, wondering what we would talk about today. Every evening I expected her to demand to see the novel, and I braced myself to tell her the truth. But after that first visit, she never asked, and I never brought it up.

And so we went on this way. It was early summer then, the days growing longer but not yet warmer. The ocean wrapped a blanket of fog thick and damp around the city and wouldn't let go. We forgot, or pretended to forget, our books. Instead we talked in our usual way—about the virus and all the uncertainty it raised, the state of the country, injustice and inequality, parenthood, motherhood, abortion—all in somewhat abstract terms, Radhika's terms. I asked questions; she answered them. It seemed this was what she needed from me. Maybe it was what she'd needed all along.

By then I knew what I needed from her: her attention, her approval. The feeling that she saw and believed in some potential in me, in what I might still accomplish.

BUT WHAT DID I need from Mercy? The question hovered like everything else—the fog, the virus—refusing to let go.

Our evenings together had begun to feel like penitentiary visits—the two of us hemmed in by the high fence, bright bulbs overhead, our faces reflected in the dark kitchen windows. I wasn't sure which one of us was the prisoner. But it was clear we were operating under false pretenses. My time with Radhika was supposedly an excuse for Mercy and me to be together, but really it was the other way around: I had used Mercy to gain access to Radhika. And now, in the fading summer dusk, our faces partially hidden behind our masks, I could see the pain and questioning in Mercy's eyes. I didn't know how to answer it.

I was in a state of true indecision. I knew I wanted to be pregnant again. Whether I wanted to go through it with Mercy—with all the uncertainty and potential disappointment it entailed—I wasn't sure. But I was no longer dead set against it. I suppose it was the loosening grip of my grief that allowed me to be drawn once again to her unblinking eyes, the soft curves of her cheeks and shoulders. I remembered what it was like to curl into her body. I longed for it.

One night after Radhika and I had been shivering on the porch for an hour and were running out of things to talk about, Mercy appeared in the kitchen window, washing something in the sink, her eyes down. Radhika stood and stretched, arms overhead, bony wrists poking out of the sleeves of her fleece. "That's my cue," she said with a wink. Then, perhaps sensing something in me—anxiety, even dread—she jabbed her chin toward the window. "What's going on with you two?"

I hesitated, mesmerized for a moment by the lift of Radhika's rib cage from her hip bones, the angular, almost weightless malleability of her body. She dropped her arms to her sides, keeping her eyes on mine, reminding me I hadn't yet answered her question. I turned and let my gaze float to where Mercy stood behind the glass, framed under the light at the kitchen sink. "I'm honestly not sure," I said.

I could sense Radhika watching me, registering my fatigue and doubt. "She's still in love with you."

I chewed on my lip. "I guess it's complicated."

"Is it?"

In the window, Mercy dried her hands and pointed to the door, her eyes a question. *Ready for me?* I felt rotten. I looked back at Radhika. "What do you think I should do?"

She held my gaze, then gave a little shake of her head, like she couldn't believe she had to spell it out for me. "I think you've got to make a choice."

I groaned and shot her a feeble smile. "I knew you were going to say that."

ONE EVENING, THE backyard once again beset by a deep fog, Mercy finally broke the silence between us. "I know you're grieving, Josie." Her hands were tucked under her armpits, her hoodie pulled low over her forehead. "And I want you to grieve on your own timeline. I'm not trying to pressure you. But I also see you opening up, in some ways. You've made a new friend. You're swimming again." She gave me a weak smile. The skin under her right eye quivered for an instant. "You're probably changing in ways I can't see, too."

I thought of my secret plans. I held my poker face.

"If you're ready for those changes, though, it seems fair to ask you to open up to me. At least a little. It's been a very ... lonely couple of months." I looked down, then back up at her. "I'm grieving, too." She blinked and raised a hand to her brow, covering her eyes, and I understood. This was what she'd been holding in, for my sake.

"Oh Mercy," I said quietly. I wanted to comfort her. I could feel myself already softening from my initial position, my determination to do it alone.

But then she said, sniffling a little, "Can I ask you something? You don't have to answer."

I said, "Sure."

She played with the strap of her mask behind her ear, "I just want you to know if you're thinking about trying again, but if it feels too scary, I would be happy to—I mean: I would even—carry it. If you wanted that?"

I stiffened. That was her solution, then: she was offering me her youthful, fertile body to fill in where my body had failed. I practically growled at her. "I'm not scared." Even though my entire nervous system, every cell in my body, tingled with fear.

She nodded like I was being the most reasonable person in the world. "Okay."

"I'm not ready to talk about it," I whispered.

She was silent for a long time, running the tip of one finger along the nylon strap behind her ear. In the distance, a mourning dove cooed its depressing cry. After a while Mercy said, "Josie, if we're ever going to recover—I mean as a couple—I'm going to need you to let me in, at least a little bit."

"That sounds like an ultimatum," I said softly, perhaps playing the part of the wounded victim more than was really fair. In truth, despite my shame and envy, I was relieved to see Mercy taking a stand, speaking up for herself. Relieved to know that if we were going to fail, it was going to be due to my own indecision and lack of resolve, not hers.

"It's not an ultimatum," she answered, her voice unwavering this time. "It's an invitation."

But I was so stuck in my own single-minded pursuit, I

couldn't see or accept what she was offering me. *An invitation to what? Your family? With its blurred lines and boundaries and super-spreader dinner parties?* Even now, when I think of how bitterly and stubbornly I resisted her, it makes me ache with remorse. "Okay," I said, purposely and unfairly ambiguous. "Thank you."

ANOTHER DENSE, FOGGY morning. A text exchange with Eleanor:

> me: So I've started swimming in the bay.
> Eleanor: !!! watch out for sharks!
> me: Haha. I will.
> me: Want to go for a walk on the beach sometime?
> Eleanor: thanks but i'm still avoiding public places.
> me: Don't you think the beach is probably safe?
> Eleanor: i don't know what's safe anymore.
> me: You sound like Radhika. Want to talk?

I pulled on my shoes and headphones, called Eleanor on speed dial and set out along Great Highway. Under my sneakers the asphalt was gritty with sand. "If you won't go outside," I said, "how are you getting any fresh air and exercise?"

"Ah, those things are overrated anyway."

I didn't laugh.

"Just kidding. Sort of. I think I can live without fresh air and exercise for a little while. Maybe I can try one of those home aerobics videos."

I couldn't picture Eleanor squatting and scissoring her legs in front of her laptop. "Any signs of rehearsals starting up again soon?"

"Nooooo. You probably know more about that than I do, anyway."

"It's true. Things are looking pretty grim from a PR perspective."

"Meanwhile, they're still not paying us."

"I'm sorry, Eleanor."

"At least I have Bach," she said with a sigh. "I can play the sonatas and partitas all day, every day, and never get bored."

"Well that's good I guess."

"Seriously though, I'm thinking about skipping town if things don't change soon. I don't have that much keeping me in the Bay Area at this point. I'm certainly not sticking around for the cheap rent."

My stomach twisted. "Where would you go?"

"Mark and I have been talking about Spokane, near our cousin. Do you know what kind of place you can get in suburban Washington for the rent you pay here for a one-bedroom? There's a pretty good chamber music community up there, apparently."

I heard myself say, "I would miss you."

"Ah, Josie. I'd miss you too." She breathed quietly into the phone. "What about you? You're going to keep plugging along with the symphony?"

"As long as they'll pay me," I said. "I still like the work. I miss going into the office."

"And your novel? Are you going to publish it?"

"Ah. Good question. Seems like the answer is no."

She was quiet for a while. Then she said, "Don't ever let yourself feel like a failure, Josie. The life of an artist is striving very hard for very little reward. It's about the process, not the outcome."

"Thanks. I know you're right." Then I added, "It seems like it might take some striving to be a mom, too. Also without any guarantee of reward—whatever 'reward' even means."

"Yes," Eleanor said. "But I imagine the same is true there. Not that I know from personal experience, obviously. I just mean: the striving might be what matters in the end. "

28

ARLY JUNE: THOSE long, breezy days when normally you would see kids huddled at bus stops in the late afternoon, their eyes blank with boredom, and it would seem right that the school year should end soon. This year there were no teenagers at the bus stops or kids walking home with their mothers. The city seemed unnaturally empty, like a vase without flowers in it. The fog made everything still and quiet.

During that time I saw almost nothing of Saniya and Sachin. Through the windows into the bright kitchen I could see their months-old art projects still stuck on the walls: shamrocks and leprechauns, rainbows emerging from pots of gold. Water bottles and markers and glue sticks lay scattered across the kitchen table, little sweatshirts and shoes on the floor. But the children themselves were nearly invisible.

Radhika and Mercy both talked about them. Radhika mostly with complaint and exhaustion. "It's still too much. Even with Mercy here, they want me for every little thing. Especially Saniya. She's become so … attached."

I tried to listen without judgment or envy. It seemed to me like it could be the loveliest thing in the world: to be needed. But then I thought of the photos lining the walls of her office, and of what Adam had said: "She's a black box."

Mercy had backed off of any attempt at emotional connection. Instead she talked in detail about the kids' development, their interests and activities. Sachin was learning to dribble a basketball. Saniya could do a hundred-piece jigsaw puzzle in thirty minutes flat. Mercy was doing online kids' yoga with them and teaching them to kick a soccer ball at the park, where the play structure was still wrapped in yellow hazard tape. "To them, this is just how it is now. They work with what you give them." They were good kids. Mercy said so all the time.

But it was also true, she said, that Saniya was getting more defiant. "Not so much with me, but with her mom. Any boundary Radhika sets, she wants to push back. It's almost like—"

"Like what?"

She thought for a moment. "It's like she's trying to break her down. Like she's asking, *If I do this, will you still love me? What if I do this? Or this? Or this?*" Mercy's face looked pained. "I feel bad for her."

"For Radhika?"

She blinked at me. "For Saniya."

THEN, JUST AS swiftly as it had rolled in, the fog burned off, and for several days the air over the ocean refused to blow its cool breath over the city. San Francisco grew warm, then one day, truly hot. All afternoon I sweated in my apartment. By the time I arrived at Radhika's house after my swim, the skin under my backpack was damp with sweat. When I pulled off my helmet, crispy triangles of hair stuck to the sides of my face.

Radhika came onto the porch in a loose tank top and shorts, all bony clavicles and bird legs. Her eyebrows were drawn together. She said something about Saniya being "a terror" all day. "If I have to interact with that child one more time tonight, I'm going to completely lose it."

She sat with her back to the door and placed two bottles of chilled water between us. They sweated on the table while we did our usual dance, both of us avoiding the work we were ostensibly there to do. We talked about a novel I was reading, which she'd recommended. She vaguely discussed a new idea for a book structure.

We'd been outside only a few minutes when I looked up and saw Saniya through the glass doors, standing still as a deer on a highway. She looked half a foot taller than when I'd last seen her and somehow more grown up. It was uncanny how much she resembled Radhika, with her high forehead and pointed chin, her black hair framing the bones of her face. In a sleeveless nightgown that hung over her narrow shoulders she looked like a ghost, like she might float through the glass doors and tap Radhika on the shoulder with one slender, icy finger. I met her gaze briefly, then snapped my eyes away, like I'd been caught in some betrayal. "Uh-oh, Rad," I said.

She must have known exactly what I'd seen. She whirled around to face her daughter, her eyes already flashing. For a long moment, neither of them moved. I felt the damp patch of sweat between my shoulder blades. A shudder passed through me.

"God damn it," Radhika whispered. She stood, opened the door and walked straight to Saniya. She said something quietly to her, placed both hands on her shoulders, and rotated her little body toward the living room, ready to march her up the stairs.

Just then Mercy appeared, looking flustered. She said something apologetic to Radhika that I couldn't make out. Radhika said something back, her voice low and calm. Then Mercy took Saniya upstairs and Radhika returned to the porch, closing the French doors carefully behind her. There was something eerily still and small about her movements, like the tiniest branches of a tree trembling before a storm.

"What did she want?" I asked, trying to sound lighthearted.

Radhika sat down. "Oh, nothing. Nothing at all. She wanted to kiss me goodnight. Even though she already kissed me goodnight."

"Ah."

"She knows the rules. She just wants to break them."

"She needs you," I heard myself say.

She clenched her jaw. "She wants me."

As she was saying it—making this fine distinction—Saniya appeared at the door once again, this time in motion, running, her arms reaching for the door handle, Mercy following a few steps behind her. "Uh-oh," I said again, but Saniya was already opening the door. In a second she was outside, panting, motionless, at Radhika's elbow.

For a moment everything stood still. From the other side of the doorway Mercy pleaded, "Come on, Saniya. Come back here." I'd never seen Mercy in the role of ineffective adult, uselessly negotiating for a child's cooperation. She seemed somehow pathetic next to the stoic determination on display. Saniya wanted only her mother, and would not stop until she got what she came for. But like a criminal or a thrill seeker, she knew the risk she was taking. Her eyes burned with the knowledge and the terror of it.

Still, Radhika stayed calm. She turned slowly, this time without rising from her chair. Her eyes were level with Saniya's. I could see them in profile now, facing each other. The cool, dry air from the house wafted out onto the porch. Mercy stood frozen in the open doorway. I tried to meet her gaze, but it was trained on Radhika and Saniya. I knew she was holding her breath, like me.

"Saniya," Radhika said, her voice as cold and slicing as a speculum blade. "Go. To. Bed."

Saniya just stared back at her mother, saying nothing.

"Now." Radhika lifted her arm, pointing one long finger toward the door. "Go."

Mercy, sounding miserable, said, "Come on, Saniya. Let's go."

But Saniya held her silence. It was the longest, most horrible silence I'd ever heard. I thought I knew how it would end. But what happened next surprised me. The sound that erupted was not Radhika's furious voice. It was a wail from Saniya so raw, so devastated and despairing that at first I didn't know where it came from. I thought some wild animal must have been trapped somewhere nearby, hurt, searching for its mother. It echoed in the thick, hot air, lasting longer than any human sound should, especially coming from a human so tiny and desperate. As it went on, tears stung behind my eyes—tears for Saniya and Radhika, for Nivea, for my dead mother, for all mothers and daughters, and for the mortal, bodily limits binding such a limitless, imperfect love. Something caught in my throat and I pressed my lips together, forcing back a cry of my own.

In the same moment, Saniya rushed at Radhika, throwing her little body at her with all her force, arms flung wide as though to wrap them around her mother's neck. But Radhika, instead of catching and holding her close, sprang to her feet just as Saniya launched herself in the air. Her small body bounced off her mother's tall, bony frame, and she fell to the porch in a heap of little-girl arms and legs and crumpled nightgown.

Radhika roared. "Enough!" She already had Saniya by the wrist and was half-lifting, half-dragging her back into the house. "Enough, Saniya. Enough of this." Saniya continued to cry out in that raw, animal wail. Tears spilled over the rims of my eyelids. It took all my strength not to run after them, to grab Radhika by the shoulders and shake her. *Stop! What are you doing? Can't you see she needs you?*

Nothing could have been a worse mistake, and I knew it. Mercy knew it too. Neither of us followed them. We just stood there and watched. Sachin had appeared at the foot of the stairs, also crying. Radhika stormed past him, shouting, still dragging Saniya by the arm so that her little feet barely touched the ground. Sachin turned and followed tearfully behind. All three of their voices—Radhika's yelling, Saniya's wail, Sachin's whimpering—faded through the ceiling. A door slammed.

In the awful, lingering silence, I stood facing Mercy. To her I must have looked as pitiful and hapless as Saniya, my hands and mouth trembling, my face streaked with tears. She seemed to be weighing what to do or say. After a long moment, she came to where I stood, glued to the spot where I'd jumped from my chair. She put her arms around me. I sank my body into hers. It was the first time I'd let her touch me in months.

Slowly, we sat back down in the chairs where Radhika and I had been sitting minutes earlier. It was still bright as day, the heat just beginning to soften under a loose breeze. It could have been any other evening, the two of us making small talk on Radhika's porch. Except we were silent, and there was a bond between us that we both knew had been missing. I clung to it even as I wanted to push it away. She held my hand. With my other arm I wiped the tears and sweat from my face. "Do you think they're okay up there?" I said after a while.

"I know they are."

"She would never—"

"No," she said. "Not Radhika. She has too much self-control."

I knew she was right.

Then she said quietly, "And she loves them too much."

While her words hung between us, I had the distinct thought that this couldn't be exactly what she meant. Because how does a mother love her children "too much"? But when I thought about it more on my long ride home, I realized Mercy was right: Radhika's problem, I was beginning to understand, was a problem of excess, of having, or being, "too much." Her passion, her generosity, her ambition. Her work, her writing, her secrets. All of it had to be contained inside one person, one lifetime. And she couldn't quite do it. No matter how hard she tried, something was always spilling over, or threatening to. Her love, and her anger, had that wild, terrifying energy of someone failing to contain the uncontainable.

Somehow I felt sure Radhika's fury would burn itself out quickly, like the hottest flame, and that despite all her rules and lines drawn in the sand, the night would end with the tenderness Saniya so desperately sought: all of them collapsed in a soft, tired heap of love and remorse. The kids sniffling, Radhika stroking their silky hair. "I'm sorry for yelling." Their tiny voices, their little shuddering breaths. "Sorry, Mama. We're sorry, too."

29

OF ALL MY conversations with Radhika, it is one of our last that remains the most vivid to me. It stands out, smooth and brilliant against the rest, like a pearl in the scooped shell of my memory.

We were in the final days of June. The whole city felt different that night. Protests over police brutality and racism had swelled to a fever pitch, and Mercy had asked Radhika permission to attend one of the marches downtown. Radhika had granted it.

I was, as usual, absorbed in my own selfish concerns. I had received an automated email that morning through my electronic medical record: *A Message from Your Doctor*. It contained an attachment of several pages filled with dense, clinical language. The autopsy report. I printed it out and brought it with me to Radhika's house. She read it silently, her eyes moving rapidly over the pages.

As she read, I asked her, "What happened to me—I mean to Nivea—is it called a stillbirth?"

"Technically, no," she answered in her doctor voice, authoritative yet gentle. "It's not a stillbirth. The term they use here, *pre-viable intrauterine fetal demise*, it's essentially a fancy term for a miscarriage."

"Miscarriage." I whispered the word as she handed the papers back to me. I held them in my hands, hardly feeling them.

She explained that the term *stillbirth* referred to a pregnancy that ended after twenty-four weeks, when the fetus could have been capable, at least theoretically, of surviving outside the uterus. "But before twenty-four weeks what comes out of a woman's body, whether it's—whether there's a heartbeat or not, is called a fetus, not a baby. It's a *fetal demise*. A miscarriage."

"Oh."

She looked at me with gentle eyes. "Most people think of a miscarriage as something that happens early, some bleeding and cramping, like a bad period, and then it's over. But you went through half your pregnancy. You were publicly, visibly pregnant. You held her in your hands. And so to you, it feels like something more. Like a death."

"Yes," I said.

We were silent for a while. The summer heat had backed off again. The evening was misty and mild. In the corner of the yard a dogwood tree was in bloom, its white flowers turned upward like tiny saucers. The words from the report still swam in front of my eyes. *Pre-viable intrauterine fetal demise. Delivered in a single container. Unremarkable tissue.* They felt as blatant and cruel as any lie.

"You want to know a secret?" Radhika said, brushing some hair from her eyes, looking intently at me. "You have to promise not to tell anyone."

"Yes," I said, holding her gaze.

"I believe life really does begin at the moment of conception." I stayed still, waiting for her to go on. "I think every woman who's pregnant is carrying a life inside her, and from that first moment, she's a mother to that life. Even if she miscarries after a few days, or even if she has an abortion. During that time, she becomes a mother."

Her voice was almost serene. All her frustration and rage, all the strain of the virus and her isolation with her kids seemed to have melted away. As I listened to her, I felt she understood me completely, and that she was the best doctor and the best friend in the whole world. I wanted to lean my body into hers and let her hold me, and cry together for the babies we'd both lost. Instead I asked the question I knew she wanted me to ask: "But if every pregnancy is a life from the moment of conception," I said, "then what is abortion? Isn't it a death? Or even a form of killing?"

"No," she said. "Absolutely not."

Again I waited for her to go on.

"That's the beauty of it." Her eyes glittered. "The beauty is in the gray area, in the contradiction. I can *believe* a pregnancy is a life, and it might be an incredibly meaningful life to the woman carrying it. But that doesn't mean abortion equals killing." I twisted my mouth to one side, pantomiming a quizzical, skeptical listener—even though I'm not sure that's what I was. When she prompted me, it was with the confident smile of someone who knew where she was going. "What? Do *you* believe abortion is killing?"

I faltered. I thought of the abortion I'd had when I was twenty-two, which I'd never once cried over. I'd never believed myself to have killed, or even to have lost, something or someone. But then I thought of Nivea, and her little body cupped in my hand, and the words on the autopsy report: *unremarkable tissue.* I thought of the pictures on the protestors' signs, the torn, bloody limbs that looked so much like her pale, intact ones. I imagined Radhika pulling those little limbs apart with her surgical tools. I thought of Amalia, and the moral of her story. *That's why abortion is killing a baby.*

"I'm actually not sure," I said. "You're so clear on so many things. You've thought them through so carefully. It's all a lot more … complicated for me. I guess sometimes I don't really know what I think."

I should have known it was the wrong answer. Her voice became defensive then, even a little hostile. Her face darkened. She breathed out through her delicate nostrils. "What do you mean, you don't '*know what you think?*'"

"I mean …" Suddenly I felt very tired. But I resolved, as I always did with Radhika, to try my best, to be as clear as I could. "I don't know what it even means: 'Choose Life.' With Nivea, I didn't get to choose. But if I could, I would have chosen life for her."

"Of course," she said. "But that would've been *your* choice. Not anyone else's."

"Well, what about all the things we can't choose? The things that just happen, or don't happen. Maybe that's what the bumper sticker is supposed to mean. 'Choose life.' Instead of trying to design and control things all the time. Just accept life as it is. Just let it happen."

She stared at me. "You really think that's a responsible way to live? Does that mean we should do away with abortion? And birth control for that matter? And all the women in the world who have virtually zero control over their lives and their bodies—should they just accept that?"

"No, of course not. I—"

"You want to just float through life, letting things happen to you? That's a privilege, Josie, to live that way."

I thought of Mercy out in the streets, fist in the air, shouting the names of the dead. I felt a surge of pride for her, and a twinge of shame for myself, hiding in the fenced safety of Radhika's backyard, still searching for her attention and approval.

We're so lucky, Radhika had said once. And it was true of me, too. Even after everything that had happened, I was in control of my life and my choices. Surely that's what Radhika would say: I was lucky. I was in control. "Well," I said, shaking my head. "When you say it like that ... I don't know, you see? I really don't know what I think."

In her gaze I felt her utter incomprehension, maybe even contempt. It radiated off her like a kind of heat. "But it's not true," she said. "You do know what you think. What you mean is, you don't understand how *other* people think. Or if they even know *what* they think. Like that man, and maybe his wife, or whoever bore and gave birth to their son. Surely they have many complex, contradictory beliefs and emotions, just like the ones you're talking about. The difference between them and you is: they sum it all up with a bumper sticker."

I said nothing, just sat there watching and listening to her.

"So *they're* the ones who don't know what they think," she said. "Not you and me. We *know* what we think."

This was what it was like to talk with Radhika. She was so certain of herself, so confident. And she was confident in me, too—more than I was in myself.

30

THE NEXT MORNING there was an email from the fertility clinic: they had reopened for insemination procedures. Without lifting my fingers off the keyboard, I clicked on the SCHEDULE link in the email. I booked the soonest appointment I could, six days away.

"Did you ever think about having another child?" I asked Carol the following evening. We were sitting near the beach after our swim, our hair wrapped in towels. The sun was still high. A breeze chilled the tips of my ears.

"I thought about it." She sipped from her thermos. "But by then Christopher's dad and I had split up. And I didn't know if I could handle being a single mom. Anyway, they didn't have the technology then like they do now. I would've had to adopt, or find a friend to get me pregnant, and I didn't know anyone like that. So I never did try again. Christopher was my one and only child."

I heard the pain in her voice, and I thought I might break in two. We were quiet for a while, looking out at the bay, seagulls squawking over our heads.

Then she said, "What about you?"

I peered down at my feet in the bucket. They looked far away under the water. "I'm thinking about it. I mean, I've pretty much made up my mind to try."

She waited for me to go on.

"But the thing is I don't know how much more I can take. I don't know if I could stand to go through it again, what happened with Nivea."

"Ah. But you can't let that be what holds you back."

"No, I suppose not."

That night lying in bed, I had the feeling I sometimes got of being back in the water, the sloshing motion of the bay lifting and rocking me, back and forth. My eyes flew open. The stillness of the room, its square corners and straight lines, hit me like a brick. I closed my eyes again, and the rocking sensation returned. I tried to let myself slip into it, float on it, make it last.

I thought of Carol, and of what she must hear and feel when she lay awake at night. The school bus bearing down on her, the sirens wailing in her ears. I turned over in the bed and grabbed onto the sheet, bunching fistfuls of it in my hands, squeezing my eyes shut, holding on as tight as I could.

A FEW DAYS later I picked up my medications from the clinic and followed the typed instructions, injecting myself each morning and again at night, after returning from Radhika's house. The following Tuesday I lay on my back, hips at the edge of the exam table, knees splayed, as the nurse slipped the syringe full of sperm through my cervix.

Afterward I lay there in the dark room. I had done it. I was here again. Alone.

After twenty minutes I stood and pulled on my skirt and sandals. In the hallway, the elevator slid open with a ping. Two women stood inside. One of them was Radhika. She was wearing her scrubs, staring down at her phone, tapping it with her long thumbs. Above her mask, her face had the modulated, almost bored look of someone going through her workday.

"Rad," I said. She didn't say anything, just put her phone in her back pocket. "What are you doing here?"

The other woman glanced back and forth between us, then edged past me toward the clinic door. Radhika stepped into the hallway. The elevator doors slid shut behind her. "Oh, just picking up some records for a patient." Her dark eyes seemed to drill into mine. "What are *you* doing here?"

This time I didn't hesitate. I said, "I was having a procedure. An insemination." I breathed the word out and felt the secret weight of it dissolve in the air between us. "I decided to try again."

The elevator pinged and the doors opened once more, but this time no one was inside. They slid shut reluctantly, like a blinking eye, watching us. "Josie," Radhika's voice was low and steady. "Are you sure that's a good idea?"

For a moment every external sensation seemed slow and amplified. A dull hum came from behind the wall as the elevator dropped away. An overhead vent forced a rush of warm, dry air down my neck. I stared back at Radhika, not moving.

What had I expected her to say? I suppose I'd thought she would be happy for me. I had this sort of vague, un-formed theory that Radhika liked seeing herself reflected in me. Like Eleanor had said. She was a writer, so she wanted me to be a writer; she was a mother, so she wanted me to be a mother. Or she had certainly seemed to want that for me, at one point. But something had changed. I had misunderstood something, miscalculated.

"I guess I thought it was obvious," I said. "I thought you would assume …"

She shook her head, a quick, dismissive flick of her jaw. "I didn't assume anything."

Suddenly I felt defensive, even angry. I had an urge to explain myself, to make her understand, and at the same time I wanted to throw up my hands, push past her into the elevator and leave, without any explanation or excuse.

Before I could decide what to do, she said in a voice that was impatient but not unkind, "Josie, I'm sorry. I can't talk about this now. I've got to get in there and get back to the hospital with these records."

"Okay." I felt a little desperate. "Maybe we can talk later? Can I still come over tonight?"

"Of course." Then she added, "You're always welcome. You don't have to ask." But her voice sounded flat and closed, like she was forcing herself to say something she didn't mean.

Still, whatever this coldness was, maybe it wasn't about me. Maybe there was some misunderstanding that I could clear up. I just needed to make her see: This is me making my choice. It may not be what you wanted or expected, but it's mine. Isn't that the whole point?

"I'll see you later," I said.

She walked past me and through the clinic door, her shoulders square, her neck long and straight. I watched her go.

THE NURSE PRACTITIONER told me to avoid swimming for at least forty-eight hours. So that evening I skipped my swim with Carol, took a hot shower at home, and rode straight to Radhika's house. As I wheeled my bike through the side gate I could see Radhika and Adam through the kitchen window. She was at the table, her laptop and some printed pages spread out around her. He said something and she looked up. When she saw me she stood and came outside.

It was one of those midsummer evenings, the air soft, the clouds high and thin in the sky. It felt good to take off my helmet and let my hair fall over my shoulders, its feathery tips on my skin.

Radhika sat across from me. Once again I noticed how tired and depleted she looked. She stared at me with her dark, heavy-lidded eyes. Then she said the same thing she'd said at the clinic: "Josie, are you sure this is a good idea?"

This time I was prepared. I took a breath and felt it tremble a little in my chest. "I'm sure it's what I want."

"And have you thought about the risks?"

"What risks?"

She blinked. "Your age, for one thing."

"You told me last time I shouldn't worry about that."

"That was before. Since then you've had a second-trimester miscarriage. Which means you're at high risk for that happening again."

"I realize that."

"Or something else could go wrong. You could have a chromosomal anomaly, or a health complication, and then you'd have to make some *really* hard decisions."

"And you think I couldn't make those decisions?"

She looked at me sternly, the way she sometimes looked at Saniya and Sachin. "You can't even decide on an ending for your novel." She must have seen me flinch, because she said more gently, "Josie, this is my job. It's what I do all the time. I can't help it if I'm thinking a few steps ahead."

I took another slow breath, and said what I'd decided to say. "You're not my doctor, Rad. It's not your job to give me advice."

She looked struck by this. Narrowing her eyes and leaning forward, she said, "It's not my job to give *anyone* advice. I give my patients information. I tell them their options. Then I let *them* decide."

"Then why are you trying to give *me* advice?"

She threw up her hands. "Because you're not my patient, Josie. You're my friend. I don't know anything about my patients' lives, all the circumstances and factors that go into their decisions. But I *know* you. I think I know you pretty well, actually. I know what's at stake for you. I drove you to your abortion twenty years ago, for crying out loud."

At that moment, a memory came flooding back: something she'd said that day as we were leaving Planned Parenthood. I'd just climbed into her car. She reached over and picked a dried wisteria blossom from my hair, as fragile and weightless as a snowflake. Looking at me with all the wisdom and certainty I so desperately craved, she'd said, *"Now you can go be a writer."*

Finally I understood. This was what Radhika believed about me. She'd never tried to hide it, had in fact been telling me so all along, only I had refused to hear her: She didn't see me as special, or even unusually capable. She thought I could only handle one thing or the other. The book or the baby. The rich, creative life or the sacrificial life of motherhood. Not both. Not like her.

I said, almost in a whisper, "What's at stake for me, Rad?"

She narrowed her eyes. "Come on, Josie. You are *this* close to finishing your novel, and you've got a big-shot agent waiting to read it. And it's *good*. It's actually good. All you have to do is *finish* it."

I would be lying if I didn't admit how much it pleased me to hear her say this. But I was too angry now to be mollified by her praise. "And who says I can't finish it while I'm pregnant? Or once I have a baby?"

At this she tipped her head back. I saw her hands squeeze into tight little fists. "Haven't you learned *anything* hanging around this house for the past year?" She lowered her head to look at me. "You don't *know* how hard it is. You cannot even *imagine*."

I kept breathing my slow, careful breaths, even as I seethed inside. "Rad," I said, "I'm sorry to tell you this. But I was never going to finish the novel. Baby or no baby. I'm done with it. I haven't picked it up since March. Since the miscarriage." She said nothing, and so I added, for emphasis: "I'm done."

She stared at me for another long moment, shaking her head. "I knew it." Then, with a rueful little laugh, "When were you going to tell me this?"

"I don't know. Eventually." I knew how pathetic it sounded.

"And what have you been doing this whole time, then? Are you working on anything?"

"Nothing in particular. I've been writing, but just for myself, in my notebooks."

"I see." Then she said with a bite in her voice, "In your diary."

I flinched, but said nothing. The silence hung between us like something dead and bloodied.

After a moment, fluttering her lashes in exasperation, she said, "Josie, we've talked about this before. I know you don't want my advice, but I'm going to give it to you anyway: Life isn't something that just happens to you. You have to *make* a life. You have to deliberately shape it and construct it. You and Mercy, you both seem to think you can just float along and somehow everything will turn out all right. Mercy's young, she's got some time to figure it out. And maybe she doesn't really have that much ambition. I still don't totally understand her, to be honest. But *you*." She shook her head again, disappointment radiating off of her like something toxic. "You have *actual* talent, and dedication, and discipline. You have worked *so* hard and you've gotten *so* close. And you can just let it all go? Just like that?"

I didn't know how to answer this, so I just stared at her. Finally she said, "Does Mercy know?"

"About what?"

"About you getting pregnant again."

I felt a flush rise to my face. "Not yet."

Her head on its long neck traced a slow, disapproving arc from side to side. "Come on, Josie. What are you doing?" She glanced at the door and the dark kitchen. Mercy was almost certainly upstairs with the kids, who were quiet tonight, back on good behavior. From beyond the fence, two voices murmured, a man and a woman strolling down the sidewalk, talking earnestly. Their voices and footsteps swelled and faded. "Mercy's got her life on hold for you. You know that, right?"

"Her life is on hold because we're in the middle of a pandemic," I said.

"You're wrong. It's on hold because there's only one thing she thinks she wants, and it's you. She's twenty-six years old, and she waits around here every night to see if you're going to show up, and once you're here, she hangs around waiting for you to play footsie with her on the porch. Meanwhile you're stringing her along in this weird pseudo-platonic relationship, because, I don't know why, because you can't decide what you want. And now you're pregnant. And you haven't even told her?"

"I'm not pregnant yet," I said.

"Right. Not yet."

"Radhika." My voice was shaking. "It's my body. You of all people should understand that. I get to decide who I tell, and when."

"I'm not arguing with that, Josie. But this is part of a larger pattern with you. You say you want to be a writer, but then you give up on your novel. You say you want to marry Mercy—or at least you want to raise a child with her. But then you go and get pregnant without even telling her. Do you know how hard it is to actually *do* all of these things that you say you want? Do you know what writers and wives and mothers have to *do*? They have to make *decisions*, Josie. Real decisions. And then they have to *follow them through*. They have to stick around, and do the hard work they signed up for, and live with all the sacrifices and all the regrets."

I felt the anger in me harden into something spiteful, almost cruel. I narrowed my eyes and arranged my lips into a tight line. "You mean like you, Rad? And all your regrets?" Her eyes flashed at me. I went on. "Why should I listen to your advice? All along I thought you wanted to build me up, cheer me on. But all you've done is shake my confidence: in my writing, my relationship, my ability to be a mother. Why would I want to be like you, anyway? You're not a writer, you're a critic. You tell me what's wrong with my work, but you're afraid to show me yours." She opened her mouth, but I cut her off. "And big deal: so you're a mother, living with all your sacrifices and your regrets." I knew I was about to go too far. But I said it anyway, everything I'd been holding in. "I don't want to be the kind of mom you are, anyway. The kind of mom who outsources her kids to make room for her own ambitions. Screaming at your daughter and pushing her away when all she wants is to be close to you. That's not being confident, Rad. That's being selfish."

As the words came out of my mouth, I saw her eyes starting to fill. Now she tilted her face away from me as one tear, clinging to its bed of lashes, crested and spilled over a sharp cheekbone.

I had done it. I felt sick. For a long time she stayed very still, blinking but not wiping away her tears. Against the strained cord of her throat, the little pulse quivered.

Finally she dropped her shining eyes to mine. When she spoke, her voice was low and hoarse. "What am I supposed to say to you, Josie?" She shook her head once, almost imperceptibly. "You don't know what you don't know."

I felt the anger flare in me again. When would she stop seeing herself as more knowledgeable than me, more capable, more special? I stood, picked up my helmet and clicked it into place, wheeled my bike out of the yard. She didn't move, or say a single word. I rode home through the soft summer evening, the fine, invisible hairs on my arms fluttering like the cilia of some one-celled creature, the air cool against my hot cheeks.

31

SLEPT FITFULLY. IN the morning I got up early and did a few inefficient hours of work, ate a sandwich and went for a walk along the beach, the sun piercing through the splintered clouds, warming my back. I thought about the night before, everything I'd said. I felt proud of myself, and sick with guilt.

Back at the apartment, I sat in the armchair, opened my computer and wrote an email to Radhika.

Dear Rad,

Over the past year you've supported me as I tried to achieve some important things: become a mother, start a romantic relationship, finish a novel. Meanwhile I've been waffling and stalling and not being totally honest with you—or maybe with myself—about what I want. I can see how this would make you feel frustrated, even hurt. I'm still feeling my way through these desires and decisions—I suppose you could call them ambitions. Not every choice I make will be the one you think is best for me. But I will try to be more honest with you, and tell you when I'm choosing not to take your advice, rather than "leading you on," as you say.

To that end: I've already written to Sarah Marshall telling her that I no longer plan to complete the novel. I can imagine this might feel like a slap in the face, but I don't mean it that way. I cannot tell you how much I appreciate all the work you've put in with me these past several months. I don't feel that the time or the work are wasted, and I hope you don't feel that way either.

As for me and Mercy: I'm really not sure what's going to happen with us. But I know I'm not trying to hurt her or lead her on. I think some relationships just go this way: there's some back and forth as two people try to figure out what they want and need. I think that's where Mercy and I are right now.

Finally, the question of another pregnancy. It's still something I want to try for, even though I don't know what lengths I'll go to, or how many disappointments I can endure. I guess I'll find out as I go along. In the meantime, I don't think I will share the day-by-day details with you, or perhaps with anyone. I believe the doctors at the fertility clinic are giving me a clear-eyed, realistic picture of my chances. If I need more advice, you will of course be the first person I ask.

Words cannot express how much I value the love and generosity you've shown me, Rad. I shouldn't have said those hurtful things to you yesterday. I wish I could take them back. I am truly sorry.

I hope you'll share your honest response with me.
Love,
Josie

I hit SEND and sat there with my laptop on my knees, watching the waves roll in and out. I felt light, but not completely free, like a sheet pinned on a clothesline, flapping in the breeze.

I took a shower and made a cup of tea. When I checked my phone less than an hour later, Radhika had written back. I read her email standing in the kitchen, a towel still wrapped around my hair:

Josie,

Thanks for your email. You're right: I do not agree with all your decisions. But you don't need my approval to live your life. It may sound silly, but I only wanted to help.

I'm so sorry you lost your pregnancy, Josie. I think about it every day.

Some things are in flux right now. I, too, have some decisions to make. We're taking the kids to the beach for a few days. I'll tell you more when we get back. Mercy is staying behind, so maybe you guys will have a chance to connect. I hope so. Both of you are dear to me.

xoxo, R

I read it twice, trying to talk myself out of feeling disappointed. I'd offered her a genuine apology, and she'd responded with some hasty acceptance and vague pronouncements about the "decisions" she had to make. I caught myself wondering what those decisions were. I assumed they had to do with the book, or perhaps whether and when she would return to her clinical work, now that the threat of the virus seemed to be waning. Or maybe she'd decided to send the twins to private school—something she was loathe to do, but it would be a way to get them out of the house, to restore some of the conditions she needed to write. Perhaps in service of her goals, it was worth it.

She hadn't said when they would return from the beach, but I knew it wouldn't be long. Radhika didn't like vacations, anyway. I felt eager to see her, but also wary of falling into the same old pattern: sitting across from her, listening to her talk, never being totally sure of my role other than to reflect her voice back to her.

But maybe it would be different now that I'd finally stood up to her. Maybe she would see me as my own person, someone who valued her friendship but didn't depend on her constant encouragement and advice. If that was really who I was. I still wasn't sure of this, yet.

I WAITED A full week for Radhika to call, but I heard nothing. Then one morning, Mercy texted: "Can we talk?"

I hadn't seen her since before the insemination and my fight with Radhika. I'd been putting her off, saying I wasn't feeling well. Now I wrote back.

me: Sure. Can you take a walk on the beach?
Mercy: I can do whatever.

I knew this meant Radhika was still out of town. Mercy was free to go anywhere, with whomever she pleased.

We met at the top of the sandy steps and walked down to the beach in silence. The afternoon had turned foggy, the wind blustery. Nevertheless, the beach was full of people. Families, people walking alone or in pairs, most of them masked. Some wore N-95s and blue hospital gloves.

Clusters of surfers bobbed in the water. A few elderly men roamed over the sand with metal detectors, heads down, like sandpipers.

We fell into step, walking briskly, far from the water's edge. The tide was out. The sand was flat and shiny.

"How are you doing?" Mercy said after a while.

"Fine." I kept my voice polite, distant. I knew she was waiting for me to say more. "How are you doing?"

Her voice had the impatient edge of an adult speaking to an uncooperative child. "Come on, Josie. I'm asking you to have a conversation."

"We are having a conversation. You asked how I'm doing. I'm fine. And I asked how you're doing."

She said, "Well my answer is going to be a bit longer. Is that okay with you?"

"Yes. Sure."

She scowled at me, then looked straight ahead. "I'm not fine. Radhika goes out of town and you disappear for more than a week, pretending you're sick when I know you're not."

"Okay," I said. "Is that all?"

"No. I also know you're trying to get pregnant again."

I pursed my lips. Anger tingled through my whole body, down to my fingers and toes. "I knew Radhika was going to tell you. I knew it."

"Well you were right. She told me."

"When?"

She shook her head like these details shouldn't matter. "Right before they left for the beach."

"I specifically told her it was between you and me."

Her ponytail whipped around her face into her mouth. She spat it out, swatting the curls away without breaking stride. "Is it between you and me?" Her voice was angry now. "Because it seems like it's between you and Radhika."

"It's between me and whoever I want," I said. "It's my body. I didn't have to tell either of you."

Our sneakers slapped the damp sand. I could hear her keeping her breaths steady, the way I'd done with Radhika. "Did I do something wrong, Josie? Did I make you angry? Did I disappoint you?"

"No," I said quietly. I was surprised at her boldness, her certainty in herself and what she'd come to say. It was a side of her I'd forgotten over the past few months while she'd been tiptoeing around me and my grief.

"You know, for a long time I thought you didn't want to talk about the miscarriage, or about getting pregnant again, because it was too painful for you. But I'm starting to think that's not it. That you don't want the relationship we used to have."

"We don't have the relationship we used to have," I said. "Because I didn't have a baby."

She shook her head. "I'm not following you."

"Wasn't that the plan? To have a baby together? Isn't that what you wanted?"

She spoke slowly. "It's not the only thing I wanted."

"Then why do you care so much if I'm pregnant or not? Do you really want to be with me, or do you just want to be with me if you're going to get a baby out of it?"

She breathed in and out. "Tell me that's not really what you think."

"Well why else should I have to keep you apprised of every little decision I make?"

"This is not a little decision, Josie." Her voice took on a sharper pitch. "It's a big decision, and I'm trying to support you."

"And I don't need support. Thank you. Believe it or not, having a twenty-two-week miscarriage wasn't the worst thing that ever happened to me. I'm forty years old, remember? I'm not twenty-six. I've lived through the deaths of both of my parents. I can handle this. Either I'll get pregnant or I won't. Either I'll have a baby or I won't. I can do it on my own. That was my plan all along."

She spoke quietly. "Is that still your plan?"

I could've told her the truth: *I don't know. I don't know what I want. I'm afraid of making it all more complicated and painful by dragging you into it. Can't you see that it just makes it harder?*

Instead I said, "Yes. That's my plan." I knew I was about to repeat Radhika's words, even though I didn't really believe them. "I don't want to be someone you're just playing house with."

She stopped walking and stared at me. "What is that supposed to mean?"

I held her stare. "I mean, you're looking for a family. For the past five years you've lived with Radhika's family, then with your sister. Then you were planning on moving in with me, but I had a miscarriage. Now you're back to living at Radhika's again."

"What do you expect me to do, go searching for an apartment in the middle of a pandemic? We live in one of the most expensive cities in the world. I'm a nanny. I work with families. That's how I make money."

"Fine. But I've lived by myself for twenty years. I don't need you or anyone else to do it with me. Baby or no baby."

She dropped her hands to her sides, searching my face, her mouth open. "So you're breaking up with me."

She sounded like such a twenty-six-year-old, I wanted to shake her. At the same time I felt a tenderness for her, and a horror at my own fierce determination. "If you want to call it breaking up, fine. I call it making decisions about my life without having to ask anyone's permission."

At this she gave me a look of pure disgust. "You sound like Radhika."

"Maybe you think that's an insult," I said calmly. "I consider it a compliment."

"Oh really?" I saw her eyes darken, and I feared what was coming. "You think Radhika is such a wonderful, perfect person? You think she's such a good friend? I'll tell you two things you don't know." She turned to face me, and I had the distinct sense that whatever I was clinging to—my last, flimsy scrap of hope—was about to dissolve right then, blow away in the wind over the gray, frothing ocean. "She knows you broke into her house. Into her office."

I stared at her. "I don't know what you're talking about."

She could've laughed at me, but she just gave a small, patient roll of her eyes, the way I'd seen her do with Saniya. Like she was tolerating the lies of a child. "Oh, no? Fine. I'll let her sort it out with you. She says she saw you as you were leaving. And that you took something. I don't know what. Something personal."

I tried to imitate her patient eye roll, her grown-up composure, but I felt false and ridiculous, a child myself. My voice, when I spoke, was thin and wavering. "What's the other thing?"

Now she narrowed her eyes and paused, almost as though she didn't want to say it. "Radhika is moving back to Chicago. In two weeks."

I squinted at her. "In two weeks?"

"They're moving in with her parents. The kids are starting private school there in August."

The wind whipped our hair in both of our faces, the sand in our eyes, so that I could hardly see her. "With her parents?" None of it made any sense.

"They want to be closer to family, to have more help. Eventually they'll buy their own place." I thought I heard a smugness in her voice: all the details she knew about Radhika's plan, a plan that so clearly excluded me, in the most terrible, final, dismissive way.

"When did they decide this?"

"She told me before they left for the beach. But it sounds like they've been thinking about it for a while."

I thought of what Radhika had said to me: *You don't know what you don't know.* "Why wouldn't she tell me?"

Mercy threw up her hands. "Why would she tell you? Radhika doesn't owe you anything. She makes her own decisions about her life. She doesn't need anyone else's permission."

I knew she was throwing my words back at me, mocking me, but I didn't care. I hardly heard what she was saying. All I could think was: *two weeks.*

Mercy went on. "She only told me because she wants me to move out before they get back from Sea Ranch." She sounded less angry, even a little sad, raw. "And so here I am, trying to figure out if I'm going to move back to my sister's house again, or thinking maybe there's a chance you would still want us to live together. But that's not what you want. I see that now."

I knew if I didn't start walking I was going to cry. I also knew I couldn't let Mercy see me cry over this: Radhika leaving. I'd gotten it all wrong. I turned and headed back toward the beach steps, which now seemed very far away. I hadn't realized how far we'd walked. I wondered if Mercy would jog to catch up, falling into step beside me, but she didn't. When I glanced over my shoulder, I saw her walking in the opposite direction, away from me, her head bent against the wind, her dark curls blowing out behind her.

$$32$$

A FEW DAYS went by. I forced myself not to contact
Radhika. But after a week, I couldn't stand it anymore. I texted her:

Hey Rad. Eager to talk once you're home. Let me know
when is good for you?

She didn't answer. I thought about texting Mercy for an
update, but I was too ashamed. I kept waiting. I remembered the time after college when Radhika stopped replying
to my emails, and it turned out she'd been diagnosed with
breast cancer. *It's not always about you, Josie.*

Several more days passed. I went to the clinic for a blood
test. I felt suddenly impatient, eager to be certain about
something, anything.

The nurse practitioner called a few hours later. "I'm
sorry, Josie," she said. "It didn't work this time. You're not
pregnant. We can try again next month, if you'd like."

The next morning I was bleeding.

I rode to Radhika's house through the sullen, foggy city. I was certain they must be back from the beach by now, if they were moving to Chicago in a week. I didn't tell her I was coming.

On my bike with the wind on my back, I felt my heart pounding in my throat. I knew I had to apologize, and I would. But it occurred to me that I should have prepared something more to present to her, some kind of plan. Whether she forgave me or not, I felt the need to reassure her that I was capable of handling my own life, that even though she was leaving, I would be okay.

But as I rode, feeling the gathering speed of my wheels on the pavement, their almost weightless precariousness, I realized I had nothing to say that would satisfy her. The plan was that there was no plan. I wasn't pregnant. I wasn't writing a book. I had spurned Mercy. If she'd been waiting around for me, as Radhika claimed, she certainly wasn't waiting any longer. Everything that had seemed within reach—a book, a baby, a family—all of it had disappeared. I felt the sad emptiness of this, not unlike what I'd felt when my baby left my body: the hollow depression at the top of my pelvis that I could still reach down and touch, a physical ache inside me. But it was also a kind of freedom—vague and elusive, but unmistakable.

That's what I would tell Radhika, the one thing of which I was certain: I didn't have to live my life the way she lived hers. I didn't have to write the ending first. *The process, not the outcome,* I imagined myself saying to her. The sureness of it coursed through me as the street sloped away and my wheels spun faster, my feet barely touching the pedals. *The story can move you. The ending can change a thousand times.*

That's a good life, too, and a good story. My mind flew briefly to Mercy, landing on her like a butterfly, then darting back to the present, to Radhika's elegant home looming on the next corner.

As I climbed off my bike I felt the hot blood under my cheeks. I flexed and extended my fingers and tried to slow my breath. Instead of wheeling my bike into the side yard, I locked it to a lamppost, climbed the steps, and strode through the front door without pausing to knock.

The house was eerily quiet. My footsteps echoed on the hardwood floor. Everything was in that strange in-between state of a family moving: rolled-up carpets propped against the walls like bodies. Closets empty, doors flung open. Bare bookshelves, boxes lining the hallways, piles of kids' clothing and toys stacked in the corners. In the dark, humming kitchen, I took the smooth square of Radhika's plum-colored shawl from my backpack and placed it on the table under the mirror, in the exact spot where it had been when she'd grabbed it like an afterthought, draping it over my shoulders. She'd never asked me to return it.

I found Adam on the back porch on a stepladder, taking down the hanging lights that had glowed over our heads all through that strange spring and summer. He told me Radhika was packing up some things at the hospital. The twins, by some miracle, were both napping. "Isn't that wild? I don't think I've seen either of them take a real nap in more than a year. Let alone both at once."

"Radhika will be bummed she missed it."

"You're so right." Then he fluttered his eyelashes in an affectionate, excellent imitation of his wife. "'You mean it was quiet for *two consecutive hours* in this house and I *wasn't there?*'"

We both laughed. Then I said, "I didn't actually know you guys were moving."

He turned away from me then, casually tugging the strand of lights off a high beam, the side of his jaw like a wall. "Yeah, I'm sorry Josie." His eyes darted down at me. "You're not the only friend who's rightly pissed at us. It was so last minute. We didn't even know for sure until a few weeks ago. But we've been thinking about it for a while. Or Rad's been thinking about it."

"I'm not pissed," I said.

He didn't seem to hear me. "It's been a hard year, obviously. I don't have to tell you that." He used the entire length of his body to twist a screw out of the beam, the muscles in his arm and trunk flexing under his shirt. A gray patch of sweat bloomed under his armpit. "Rad's been trying to write this book, and it's impossible for her to get anything done with the kids at home, and on top of that she's not been feeling well." He wiped his forehead with the back of his arm. "So we finally caved. Going to live with her parents. We'll see how long we last before we look for a place of our own. But they've got space for us, and time to help with the twins. Northwestern is giving Rad a new, better appointment, with some protected time to write, and an office. It'll be a good setup for her."

"And what about for you?"

He tugged at a screw. "Oh, I can work from pretty much anywhere, now. That's one good thing to come out of all this. I'll set up a little home office, eat my mother-in-law's home-cooked Indian food. I'm getting a great deal out of it."

He dropped his arms and looked down from the stepladder. He was smiling, but his eyes looked tired. For the first time I noticed the loose skin around his throat and mouth, the subtle hunch at the base of his neck—the spine of someone who sat at a screen all day. I saw the strain of his optimism, his constant flexibility and equanimity, his willingness to roll with every punch. It must have been hard on him, always following Radhika's lead, going along with her unilateral decisions. Or maybe he liked it that way. Maybe theirs was the kind of balance that made a marriage work.

"Well, I really hope it's a good move for you guys," I said. "For the kids most of all."

"Thanks, Josie." He scratched at the back of his neck, squinting under the midday sunlight. "You always hope you're making the right decisions for them, you know? It's a big change. But they're adaptable. Way more adaptable than adults. And for the little one Chicago will just be home, I guess." He looked a little mystified. "Born in a pandemic. What a world they're getting from us, right?"

I nodded slowly, registering his words. Then I said, "Wait—who was born in a pandemic?"

He blinked. "The baby."

I stared back at him. Then it must have crossed my face like a cloud.

"Oh jeez," he said. "Ahh. She hasn't told you?"

I furrowed my brow. "No."

"Dammit. Sorry. I'm terrible at this." He rubbed a hand over his hair. "Radhika's pregnant." He said it as calmly and matter-of-factly as if we were talking about bubble wrap or moving vans.

"Pregnant," I said.

He flopped his hands at his sides. "Sorry. I fucked that one up. She's been so careful about keeping it quiet. But she would have told you soon anyway, I'm sure."

I swallowed, remembering how pale and tired she'd looked at our first meeting on the porch, how she still looked. "How pregnant is she?"

He gave the proud, befuddled smile of an expecting father, crossed with expectation and worry. "She's due in December. So that makes her, what? Five months now?"

"Oh, wow. Five months." I felt like I couldn't get enough air. "Well. Congratulations."

"Thanks, Josie." Then he said, "Hey listen, I'm sorry for blurting it out like that. You know how thoughtful Rad is about everything. I'm sure she wants to tell you herself. Especially because of your—because of what happened with your pregnancy. That's probably why she waited. She just wanted to tell you the right way."

"Yes," I said. "I'm sure that's it."

BY THE TIME I left their backyard, the wispy clouds had hardened over the sky like an eggshell. Pedaling uphill, the wind in my face, I felt like I'd merged with the bike; I was a machine moving a strange, unknowable body through the world.

Only then did it occur to me that she must have had it all planned out, for a long time. There was no other way, no possibility of an accident, because she didn't have any of her own eggs inside her. She had only the seven frozen embryos in the fertility clinic, the clinic that had closed at the same time as everything else, the same time I lost Nivea. The day Mercy called her to the hospital, the day Radhika delivered my dead baby, she'd already made her plan. She'd already started it.

I thought of the afternoon a few weeks earlier when I'd seen her coming out of the clinic elevator, and my face burned. Picking up a chart for a patient. Bullshit. She was the patient. She'd been going there all along, all this time, and she'd been too much of a coward to tell me.

At home I went to the desk drawer where I kept my few mementos of Nivea: my hospital bracelet, a thumb drive of my twenty-week ultrasound images, the autopsy report. The strip of five photos from my very first ultrasound, and the sixth—the one I'd given to Radhika, then stole back from her.

I held that sixth photo beside the others. It was clear, as clear as anything, that it didn't belong. The paper was a different shade of white. The top edge didn't align with the smooth slice I'd made at the bottom of the others. It was finely serrated where someone—Radhika herself—had torn it off the little printer on the ultrasound machine. And when I looked closely at the image, which I'd never actually done, I could see that the embryo was smaller, and a slightly different smudged shape, like someone else's thumbprint. In tiny white letters where my own strip of photos bore my name and Nivea's due date, there was a different due date: December 2. Radhika's.

It was her photo I'd stolen. Her baby.

I grabbed my face in my hands, dug my fingernails into my cheekbones until I could feel them breaking the skin. Then I pulled them away slowly. I stood there breathing in and out for a long time.

Finally I yanked the cap off a fine-tipped Sharpie and pressed the single square photo against the desk. In the white border underneath the due date, in neat block letters, I printed a message, five short words.

THE NEXT DAY when Radhika still hadn't called, I biked by their house on my way home from the Dolphin Club.

It didn't feel like a deliberate detour; I just took my usual route as though I were stopping to chat with Radhika before riding the rest of the way home. I had her ultrasound photo in my backpack; I'd intended to return it to her, along with the message I'd written on it. But the house was dark. Even the landscape lights had been switched off. A realtor's lockbox, that universal symbol of a home without a family, hung from the front door handle.

They were gone.

PART FOUR

33

THE MONTHS HAVE passed quickly since then. Fall arrived early, then Thanksgiving and Christmas. Winter in California, clear and crisp and slate colored. Then a new year, a new vaccine, a new president. In many ways it feels like a new beginning. In other ways, not much has changed.

The JCC pool reopened, but they've got a reservation system now: one swimmer per lane, forty-five minutes at a time. No more aqua classes, no more ladies chatting and floating in the shallow end with their pool noodles.

One Saturday, resting between laps, I saw the man from Target and his son. They were walking side by side, the son with his goggles strapped over his squinting eyes, trunks stretched around his abdomen, a few thick hairs sprouting from his upper back. The father murmuring something in his ear, cautious and tender and stern, just like that day in the parking lot. I couldn't tell if it was their first time here or their thousandth. It occurred to me that maybe I'd seen them here before, without ever noticing them. I put my goggles on and swam for a while longer, occasionally glancing sideways under the water. The father kept up a smooth breaststroke as the son doggy-paddled up and down the other half of the lane. Something about the son's body under the water reminded me of Nivea. His large forehead. The sort of alien curves of his body. After a while I got out of the pool. I never went back.

That was the weekend before Thanksgiving, several months ago, now. Mercy invited me to Daniela and Steve's place for Thanksgiving dinner, and I accepted. Her family welcomed me as they had before. After dinner she and I talked for a while, and once again I felt that magnetic pull toward her—the urge to tell her something, everything. My sighting of the father and son at the pool was still fresh in my mind. But to tell that story I would've had to start with the night in the Target parking garage, and the bumper sticker—all of which seemed off-limits because it was about Radhika, and how in the end she'd left me behind, even though I'd prioritized her over everything else, over Mercy. I knew this sort of admission—my remorse, my confusion—was exactly what I owed her. I turned the words over, trying to form them in my mouth. But I couldn't do it.

We talked about other things while we nibbled our pie-crusts, the rest of the family wandering away from the table, clearing plates and coffee cups. She admitted to feeling a little claustrophobic at Myra's house. The girls were getting older and too cool to hang out with their aunt; they'd rather be on their phones. She was thinking about moving out, though it didn't seem like she'd done anything about it. I thought about how close we'd come to living together. In some ways I could still imagine it.

She asked me about the novel, and I told her I'd dropped it, even dropped the connection to Sarah Marshall. She smeared a streak of pumpkin pie filling across her plate with her fork, then looked up at me with a smile that was a bit playful but mostly sad. "I never got to read it."

I'VE TALKED TO her a few times since then. We met for coffee once at a place near Myra's house. We even went for a walk on the beach, on a day in April that was as cold and clear as the Arctic. I told her I haven't given up on trying to get pregnant again. I wasn't sure how she would react to this, but it felt like something I wanted her to know, or in any case that I didn't want to keep from her. She beamed at me. "That makes me really happy, Josie."

I've kept swimming in the bay with Carol. There are rumors the Dolphin Club might reopen in the summer, and when it does, I plan to get a membership. In the meantime, Carol's become a real friend—maybe the only friend I'll have left here, soon. We talk about the same kinds of things Radhika and I used to talk about, but with an honesty and a reciprocity I never felt with Radhika. "You know," she said recently, her hair wrapped in a towel, steam rising around us from the buckets at our feet, "I have this therapist. She's about your age, late thirties, maybe forty. And ever since I've known her, I keep waiting for her to tell me she's pregnant. Not just waiting for it—hoping for it."

I considered this. "Why, do you think?"

She shook her head. "That's the thing, I don't know. Is it some kind of grandmother instinct? Do I just like her, and think she'd be a good mom?" She sipped from her tea. "She's always worn a wedding ring. When we used to meet in person I would scan her body for any sign of a bump. Now we meet online, so I only see her from the shoulders up. I keep expecting her to surprise me one day by saying, 'I'm going out on maternity leave! I'll be back in a few months.'"

Something about this bothered me. "She might not even want kids," I pointed out.

"Right. Of course not. I just can't stop hoping she will." She shook her head again, as though to jostle the hope loose.

I leaned my elbows on my knees. I wondered whether I would ever be the kind of mom who went around wishing motherhood upon other women. Or the opposite, someone who believed that other women (certain women?) shouldn't have kids, shouldn't even try. *I know what's at stake for you.* What made Carol so different from Radhika, thinking she knew what was best for someone else, or what would make them happy?

"You said she's nearly forty?"

"Yes. 'Running out of time.' That's what they would've said in my day."

"My mom had me when she was forty-two."

Carol raised her eyebrows. "Did she."

"Yep." I looked down. "And then she died fourteen years later. And now neither of us has each other."

Carol's creased, kind face pinched together in sadness. "Oh Josie." She reached out and cupped my cheek in her hand. "I know. I know exactly. Cruel and unfair. There's really no word awful enough to describe it."

The water lapped at the sand and I twirled my tea bag in my thermos. Carol said, "It's strange, isn't it? You have something for such a short period of time—a family, a child, a life. And even after it's gone, and all the pain, still you can wish it upon others. You wish it for the people you love most of all."

ELEANOR AND I BOTH got our vaccines in January. Exactly two weeks later she invited me over for hot pot. Even vaccinated we sat six feet apart, each with our own individual bowl of broth. From the far end of the counter she told me her news: she was leaving the city. The symphony still claimed rehearsals and concerts would resume in the summer, once vaccines had been widely distributed and musicians and audiences felt "safe." But they'd made promises before, and Eleanor no longer believed them. She and Mark had rented a house in Spokane, not far from their cousin. "It just makes sense. That's why our parents sent both of us here—not just for the opportunity, but so we could be here for each other after they were gone." They planned to join a local chamber orchestra. "I've talked to the conductor a couple of times. They're gearing up to re-start rehearsals over the summer—masked, at some out-door amphitheater in the woods. Doesn't that sound so Washington?"

"And you feel comfortable with that? I mean, with in-person rehearsals? And concerts?"

She shrugged. "If I want to play music with other people, I guess I'll have to get comfortable with it."

Her brother would continue teaching his local cello students over Zoom until he could establish a new studio in Spokane; maybe he would teach lessons on their back porch. "Who knows, maybe I'll teach some lessons, too."

"Really?"

"I would think about it. I used to like teaching. But no kids." She made a little face. "Even Mark doesn't want to teach kids anymore. Too much work. Too many germs."

I laughed at this. "I'm glad for you, even though I'll miss you. I guess you've got to follow your dream."

"Sure, my dream." She looked down at the counter, then lifted her eyes and stared straight at me. "It's more like … At some point we need to stop looking everywhere for our missing parents and just … build a family of our own. Right?"

I held her gaze. "Sure," I said. "Right."

"Which reminds me." She lifted a strip of duck, turning it carefully in the broth until it was brown on both sides. "Is Mercy still thinking of starting her own music studio?"

I looked down. "I don't know."

"Well, do you think she'd be interested in taking on the half-dozen kids who've stuck with Mark over Zoom? He'll need to hand them off to someone. I bet the kids would love her. The parents, too."

I fumbled with my chopsticks, grasping for a sliver of slippery duck. "Honestly, I don't really know what's next for Mercy. But you should ask her. She'd be honored that you thought of her." I gave her Mercy's phone number. But I didn't ask her if anything came of it.

IT'S BEEN A few months now since Eleanor moved away. She sent me some pictures of their home, a shingled craftsman on a shade-dappled street, a large bay window overlooking a wooded slope. Through the glare on the glass, you can see Eleanor and Mark's music stands in the window, proud and upright, like watchmen. Trusted companions.

I miss her, worse even than I imagined. But I get the sense she's happy there, and that makes me happy, too. I think of all the work and the sacrifice her parents made to get her to San Francisco, all the hope they placed in her. It's probably hard for her to parse, now, which ambitions are hers and which came from them, and which ones really matter to her anymore. But she has a good life, even if it's a different life than what she and her parents imagined. A peaceful home in the wooded Washington suburbs, a light-filled room where she can practice her violin and look down over the treetops. Just her and her brother, their cousin nearby. A small family. It could be enough to make someone happy. Enough for any child of mine, anyway. Eleanor has already promised me—should it ever come to that. It is more than enough.

$$34$$

NOW IT'S LATE May. San Francisco is in its fullest expression of spring: white blossoms on the trees and dusting the sidewalks down Taraval Street. Squirrels chattering, burying their acorns in Golden Gate Park. The surfers out on the ocean in the mornings, watching the waves, waiting for their next move. I like to think I know a little bit about what their life is like out there. I imagine the Pacific Ocean feels something like the Bay: the cold water getting a tiny bit warmer, month by month, as we inch once again toward summer. It gets easier and easier, every afternoon, to wade into the water, and I find I'm able to stay out there longer. Maybe, as Carol says, I'm getting stronger.

The days are stretching, too. Biking home in the evenings up Arguello, pumping hard on the hill, I have to squint against the sun. By the time I lock my bike and climb the stairs to my apartment I'm hungry for my simple dinner— eggs and a salad, some fruit. Then I sit in my armchair, writing in my notebook, watching as the fog settles on the ocean like a shawl over the city's tired shoulders. I don't write about anything in particular except what I'm thinking about, whatever happened that day. This, too, feels like enough.

And once again, I'm pregnant—for now, anyway. I gave up trying for several months after Radhika left, then started again. Two more rounds of IUI didn't stick, but then finally, a few months ago, one did.

I'm only at the twelve-week mark—still in that arbitrary, anxious window of the first trimester. I tell myself I won't really feel secure until after I pass twenty-two weeks. Then I'll be able to relax, tell a few people, maybe even Mercy. Or maybe not. But I've stopped trying to temper my excitement, to pretend I can protect myself from the pain of disappointment. Some things happen. Some things don't.

I'm seeing a new doctor; she seems to take our visits very seriously. She calls me "high risk" because of my age and what she calls my "history." I go to her office every few weeks for an ultrasound. "Just to make sure everything's okay," she says. I don't mind. I like the frequent appointments. I think of what Radhika once told me about how she used to ultrasound herself in her office, just to put her mind at ease. Still, when the doctor slides the probe over my belly in its slick coat of gel, I try to think of what Eleanor would say, and Carol: *The process, Josie, not the outcome. Trust your body. Float.*

Sometimes, though, every once in a while, I hear another voice in my ears. *It's my job to think about the risks. It's my job to think one step ahead.*

I can't help it: I start to think one step ahead, too. What if I lose this pregnancy? What will I do then?

The answer is: I don't know. I don't know what I'll do.

But I'm here anyway, back in my armchair at the wide, west-facing window, my feet propped on the ottoman, my palms resting on the space between my hip bones, where sometimes I think I detect a slight movement—like bubbles, or bird's wings. Of course it's too soon to feel anything, but the idea comforts me.

I never picked up the novel again. It's been long enough now that I'm fairly certain I never will. Maybe I'll write a different novel someday. Maybe not. For now I have plenty of other material to make use of: all the events and happenings of the past year, and all that could still happen in the future.

Radhika's baby was born last December. I was surprised to get an announcement in the mail, a picture of a wrinkled, fuzzy brown creature. Archana Laurel Chevalier. On the back, a picture of their whole family: Adam hovering, thrilled and smitten and tired; the twins looking tentatively happy. And Radhika, standing slightly apart from them, baby in her arms, looking thin, proud, radiant even in her postpartum exhaustion.

Mercy texted me that day.

Mercy: You get the card from Rad?
me: Yes, she's done it again. With her usual grace.
Mercy: Ballsy of her to send it to you, no?
me: Totally in character.
Mercy: Ha
Mercy: You ok?
me: Both/and, I guess.

From the envelope, I copied down their return address in Chicago, thinking—or pretending—that I would finally return her ultrasound photo. But I couldn't bring myself to do it. Instead I left it on the wall over my desk, where I'd stuck it with a thumbtack the day they left. I see it every day.

Archana. She's already five months old by now. Presumably Radhika has gone back to work, pumping breast milk in between abortions, gazing seriously and sincerely into her patients' eyes. *It's not my job to tell you what to choose. It's my job to trust you with that choice.*

I really believe she's good at the work she does. She wasn't particularly good at it with me. But as she said, I was different. I was her friend, not her patient.

I still think of us that way: as friends.

35

TODAY I WOKE up to an email from Adam in my inbox. It caught me by surprise; I felt my heart beating the way it used to when I'd get an email from Radhika back in grad school. It's a straightforward, stoic message, obviously distributed to many contacts at once. I'll admit, even that feels like a slight. I'm aware of still wanting them—her—to think of me as special.

I shouldn't be shocked by his message, but I am. Which just shows, despite all my faithful watching, how blind I've been all along. How willing to be deceived.

Dear friends,
I'm writing with some news that we knew we'd have to share one day, although we've managed to delay it longer than we ever dared to hope.

Radhika's cancer has come back. For nearly fifteen years it's been hiding in her body, too tiny to be detected by the scans, but there nonetheless. We've had our eyes open. The doctors warned us that it would just be a matter of time. Now that time has come.

We knew, too, that another pregnancy came with the risk of hastening this inevitable end; the doctors say this is almost certainly what happened. But Radhika never wavered: this was her choice. It was what she wanted. And now that Archana is here with us, it's impossible for me not to support her, even though I am all too aware of what I—all of us—will lose.

Radhika has been given six months to a year to live, while she undergoes "palliative" chemotherapy—treatment that will ease her suffering, but will not prolong her life. She is now officially under the care of hospice. Her oncologists will guide the chemo as long as it seems to be of some use for her.

Saniya and Sachin, who will turn six in June, are bearing this new reality with remarkable strength. Archana, now five months old, remains healthy. She will nurse for a few more days until the start of the chemotherapy. Then she'll be weaned and take the bottle, which she seems prepared to do without too much complaint.

Finally, a request: Radhika is, understandably, overwhelmed by the sheer number of tasks required to merely get through each day. Once the chemo starts, she'll have little energy for anything else. She asks that you use the link below for updates on her care, which I will post regularly. And I promise to be in touch with you again when we reach the end of her remarkable, beautiful, intentional life.

With love and thanks,
Adam

I've been sitting here in the armchair since I read it, staring into space, my coffee going cold on the desk. In the glare of the reading lamp, against the milky morning sky, I can see myself faintly reflected in the glass.

I keep looking back at those words: *as we knew would happen one day.*

They knew. She knew all along. Of course she did. She just didn't want to admit it—to me, to anyone, to herself.

After a while I get up and glance over the counter into the kitchen, where my bicycle leans against the wall. I'd been planning on cleaning it this morning, hoping to sell it, upgrade to a newer, lighter model: Adam's idea. He teased me more than once about my clunky old hybrid, telling me how much easier I could get around the city on a titanium bike—the kind you can buy used for a decent price, if you're willing to watch and wait until opportunity strikes. I should have at least a few months left of cycling around town, carefully, if all goes according to plan.

Not knowing what else to do with myself, I pick up a pile of rags and sit cross-legged on the kitchen floor, a bottle of chain grease at my knee, my whole body throbbing with this new, crushing reality.

It makes everything so much clearer. That afternoon in Crissy Field, Adam's bitter resistance to my questions. Our former classmate's knowing, grim prognosis, which I—and apparently Radhika—dismissed so easily. *Every limit, shattered.* The undeniable truth of her frail body, shriveling around her like a shell that whole long spring and summer. *You don't know what you don't know.* Maybe she didn't know either, at the time. But she would've known it was coming, sooner or later.

This was always Radhika's problem, then: the unsolvable dilemma of time—her limited, precious time. She loved

Sachin and Saniya, certainly, and she wanted to make the most of her time with them. And yet she didn't want to give them all her time. She had her other passions and ambitions, for which she needed not only time, but space, solitude, energy. For her there was no "later," no "once they're a little older." Yes, they would grow up. But by then she would already be gone.

Wiping a Windex-soaked rag over the steel handlebar, watching that satisfying streak of ammonia flash and recede, I think how even the smallest, solitary task—cleaning an old bicycle—is a privilege of leisure reserved for the childless, like myself. I imagine, vaguely, a toddler at my side, careening around the kitchen. The spilt grease, the tipped bike, the spinning wheel. *Watch out! Careful. Look what you've done.* But even that is too simple. Despite what she said to me after my abortion—*now you can go be a writer*—she couldn't really have believed that was how it worked, at least not for someone like her.

Time wasn't her only problem. It's about something else, something unmeasurable. This is what I've been trying to figure out since reading Adam's email, several hours ago now. Running a rag over the chain, link by link, watching the grease work its way into the spinning gears. At some point—shortly before my miscarriage, as I've roughly calculated—she walked into that fertility clinic and convinced her doctors, undoubtedly against their advice, to implant another embryo inside her body, hastening her own death in the service of creating another life, a third child whom she would barely know. On the surface it seems like an act of surrender. But I am beginning to think maybe it was the opposite. Like Amalia's story about her son, the erroneous ultrasound, and her doctors' well-intended advice. Maybe this was Radhika's way of maintaining a sort of control and authorship over her life. It was, and is, a story written in reverse, starting from the only ending she knew.

Still. She must have her doubts, and her fears. In these remaining months, as she hooks a pinkie into the corner of her daughter's mouth and slips it off the nipple for the last time—can she be sure, now?

Maybe it's an unfair standard to hold for any decision, for anyone. Like Radhika said: *What if this? What if that?* Those questions don't really get you anywhere. It doesn't really matter, in the end.

And so, even through my own horror and sadness, I suppose I'm thankful that Radhika's doctors were willing to offer her this radical trust, to let her make her own decisions about the uses of her body. To write her own ending. Part of that ending is this: three young children without a mother. As an orphan, I dwell on that part. But I also know there's more to the story than that. Radhika has lived a brave life. She's helped many, many people. And one day she'll touch even more people, when her book comes into the world.

As for this choice, her own bold and intentional ending—I can't decide whether it's brave of her, or cowardly. I suppose it depends on who is telling the story.

LATE MORNING. I'VE left the bike in the kitchen, collected all the dirty rags and thrown them in with the week's laundry. Forced myself to eat a few bites of lunch. Now I'm back in the armchair, hands on my belly, feet on the ottoman, listening to the whir and chug of the washing machine in the hallway closet. Watching the sun cast its familiar, slanted parallelograms across the floor.

Sitting here, I've finally opened a fresh notebook to write it all down, to make meaning of it as best I can: the nature of choice, and ambition, and endings. On the wall over my desk, next to the framed picture of me and my parents, my eyes land on Radhika's ultrasound photo, and the message I wrote in its white border, a message whose layered meaning she could never have known. But I know it: YOU'RE NOT ALWAYS VERY NICE.

It's true, she wasn't. Neither was I—not to her, and not to Mercy.

My mind snags there, on an invisible countercurrent. Mercy. What is she doing now? Maybe teaching a cello lesson in Myra's backyard, surrounded by the potted lemon trees and wild, wiry lavender and the drift of the late afternoon fog. Adjusting a little elbow or wrist, training a young ear to pitch and rhythm, teaching the foreign language of notes on a page. I think about texting her, but decide against it. I know she'll write as soon as she sees Adam's email.

I find myself wondering if it's too late for us. If I can still choose her.

In one strange, almost sickening wave, I remember a story my father once told me. The memory must have been lodged somewhere dark and hidden, because it feels at once fresh and achingly familiar, as though I've been telling it to myself forever. It's a story about my mother—or rather, about them, and how they finally ended up together after years of tender, enduring friendship. I can hear my father's voice in my head, repeating the tough-loving advice of his best friend: "Every day you don't marry her, Jeff, you're taking a risk."

Of course. It's that simple. *The day nothing changed. The day everything changed.* If you're not careful, they can be the same thing.

Yes, this is what I think: life happens to us. For so many people—women in particular—this can be the saddest, most tragic truth in the whole world: Life and choice, at least some of the time, have nothing to do with each other. But I have the opportunity to make some choices, to take some risks. They may not be the same choices or risks that Radhika—or anyone else—might want for me. But that was Radhika's freedom, and this is mine. My own beautiful gray area. It is proof, more than anything, of how lucky I am.

Out on Taraval the fog is blowing in thick and the L bus is wheezing to a stop on the corner. I tuck my head against the wind and start walking. I'm ready to tell Mercy about all of it, all the questions I still have, with and without answers, the way she asked me to do from the very beginning: This pregnancy and what it will become. The man and his son and his bumper sticker. CHOOSE LIFE. The ultrasound photo on my wall, what I almost did with it, what I can never do with it now. I want to tell her what she already knows, and what my mother knew: I'm not always very nice. I want to ask her to forgive me, as I have forgiven Radhika.

Most of all I want to show her my notebooks—my diaries, as my mother and Radhika called them. But I call them something else. A story. Whatever they are, I want her to read what I've written.

Somewhere another jackhammer blasts asphalt into the cool city air. I'm walking faster now with a long, eager stride toward Mercy's sister's house, my phone and a stack of notebooks heavy in my bag, thumping against my thigh with every step.

Acknowledgments

I am grateful to the friends, editors, and professionals who read and offered invaluable feedback on early versions of *I Trust Her Completely:* Allyson Sutkowi-Hemstreet, Verlyn Klinkenborg, Alexandra Enders, Anne Matlack Evans, Angela Pneuman, Jana Luft, Mohit Mehtani, Sabina Henneberg, Elizabeth Wildman, and above all my agent, Joy Harris, whose brilliant attention and care were transformative for the manuscript and the writer.